GARY J. SHIPLEY

THITHOGS

https://cloak.wtf

© Gary J Shipley 2023

Published and Designed by CLOAK

THE HOUSE INSIDE THE HOUSE OF GREGOR SCHNEIDER

GARY J. SHIPLEY

I enter the house inside the house alone.

I make my way through a kitchen and a living room inside another kitchen and another living room, up to the claustrophobic bathroom and bedroom inside another bathroom and another bedroom with no windows on the first floor, and down to the dark spaces in front of more dark spaces of the basement inside a basement.

There is the same downbeat furniture and décor in front of décor, the same marks in front of marks on the carpets and walls on top of carpets and walls, the identical bland magnolia over bland magnolia and wood-panelled hallways inside wood-panelled hallways.

I open a fridge inside a fridge (processed cheese triangles inside other cheese triangles, bottled gherkins inside bottled gherkins), rattle through two layers of bead curtain into another living room inside a living room and sit on a brown sofa containing another brown sofa. The last two rooms inside rooms are the same, down to the smallest details: the same number of cigarette ends inside cigarette ends in the ashtrays one on top of the other. There is the same jar of Vaseline inside another jar of Vaseline and the same slimming pills inside different sleeping pills in the bathroom cabinet in front of the bathroom cabinet. The same spot wiped clean on the wall at the turn of the stairs lays over another exactly similar spot wiped clean on a wall behind a wall at the turn of the stairs behind the turn of the stairs, the same cloying, unhealthy smells and viscous puddles hide in other smells and puddles in a basement inside a basement. But they are not exactly identical.

Still no framed photographs of loved ones, keepsakes, kids' pictures over pictures and scribbles over scribbles. But there are children here, somewhere or other. I hear a baby crying from inside another baby, inconsolable and far away, when I go down to a basement beneath a basement—unless it is just the wind howling in the flue inside the flue. There is another room inside a room down there, with unopened packs of kitchen towels, biscuits, lollipops, stacked like gifts or as if for a game in front of more unopened packs of kitchen towels, biscuits, lollipops. I see a safety gate in front of a safety gate at the top of the stairs above the stairs, the baby's changing mat in a bedroom inside a bedroom. And the layers of sexual graffiti, spied through a keyhole in front of a keyhole, in an attic inside an attic. There is a child inside a child wrapped in a black plastic bag inside a black plastic bag in a bedroom inside a bedroom.

There is a landscape painted over a landscape turned to a wall in front of a wall against a living room wainscot on wainscot. And nail holes inside nail holes, and nails on top of nails without pictures inside of pictures in a hall corridor wall in front of a hall corridor wall. It is as though pictures inside of pictures are prohibited here. But the house inside the house—renovated, refurbished, restored and distressed to an exact pitch of wear and use and unwholesomeness as that renovated, refurbished, restored and distressed to an exact pitch of wear and use and unwholesomeness lying beneath it—is full of forbidden images of forbidden images. In fact, the entire house inside the house is an image inside an image, a duplicated duplication, living image of an image of itself in front of itself and its occupants inside occupants, whose stairs within stairs I tramp, whose threshold over a threshold I cross or recoil from, whose basements inside basements I crawl about in.

The more I know about what I know, the worse the worseness gets.

It is difficult not to project a narrative inside a narrative as I go up and down the stairs over stairs, step into a malodorous and malevolent bedroom inside a malodorous and malevolent bedroom, its cloying bower of nasty textures over nasty textures, grim wallpaper over grim wallpaper, gilded fittings around gilded fittings and a mirrored fitted wardrobe in front of a mirrored fitted wardrobe. Who is the child inside the child in a corner inside a corner, sitting between a bed and a wall in front of a wall, a bin bag over a bin bag that rustles as it breathes? I nudge a foot outside a foot to see if it is real.

Water's running in a bathroom inside a bathroom. The house inside the house is brought to life in the squeak of a dishcloth around a dishcloth on a wet plate on a wet plate, a cough after a cough in a distant room inside a room, the tink of cutlery, the pained groans as of a man inside a man masturbating. As if the setting inside the setting itself weren't enough—the dour brown-and-cream paintwork over dour brown-and-cream paintwork, a soulless emptiness inside a soulless emptiness, a meagre pleasurelessness at the pleasurelessness of it all.

There's nothing here to alleviate the stultifying air of boredom and implied violence, save copies of copies of the Sun and telly guide. In a basement inside a basement a cot mattress inside a cot mattress is carefully laid in a coal hole inside a coal hole.

The house inside the house is a labyrinth inside a labyrinth of insulated, soundproofed rooms inside rooms—rooms inside rooms for every imaginable and unimaginable purpose inside rooms inside rooms for every imaginable purpose. Rooms inside rooms for a living death, with walls in front of walls built in front of walls in front of walls, pointless corridors inside corridors, blind windows in front of blind windows, rotating rooms inside rotating rooms and rooms inside rooms from which, if you are accidentally locked in, there is no escape.

The leaden atmosphere is too familiar to me: a timbre of a timbre of extreme sadness about sadness, repressed feelings about repressed feelings, secrets about secrets, the unspoken unspokeness.

I can't avoid the avoidance of myself in here. My living of my life, like some dreadful trauma about trauma, is endlessly replayed without resolution or consolation.

I enter rooms inside rooms only to experience another uncanny twin of a twin. It is sinister in its little details inside details: like dirty mattresses around dirty mattresses, and little cracks in the walls in front of cracks in the walls.

As a latch over a latch on a door in front of a door to a small room inside a room quietly clicks shut, leaving me alone in the gloomy light behind the light, a queasy sense of trepidation sets in. Walking down a carpeted hallway inside a carpeted hallway, I can hear the sound of dishes being rewashed in an adjacent room inside a room. Faced with the choice of entering and proceeding either up the stairs outside the stairs or, worse, down into an even murkier basement inside a basement, I pause by a door in front of a door, take a deep breath and enter and enter again.

Behind a door behind a door is another kitchen inside a kitchen that leads through beaded curtains behind beaded curtains into another dingy, stale living-room inside a living room. With no response to my 'hello! hello!' I feel invisible twice over. I rummage through cupboards in front of cupboards, drawers inside drawers and shelves that are shelved.

Grimy flock wallpaper over grimy flock wallpaper chokes the rooms inside rooms. Shabby thick brown carpet over shabby thick brown carpet smothers floors on top of floors. Every detail, down to the last cheap brass drawer handle, is pure British kitchen-sink-inside-kitchen-sink misery. Upstairs, is another clammy, humid bathroom inside another clammy, humid bathroom. In a bedroom inside a bedroom another small figure around a figure sits calmly inside a bin liner inside a bin liner. A small mattress on a mattress in another putrid-smelling basement inside a basement suggests some second layer of unspeakable abuse.

In the grim, tobacco-stained tobacco stain oppressiveness of a room inside a room are plastic carrier bags full of plastic carrier bags full of identical items, books around books stacked in exactly the same way. There are giant cages inside cages: 3 x 3 metre cells inside cells containing an air mattress in an air mattress, a beach umbrella inside a beach umbrella and a black plastic garbage bag inside a black plastic garbage bag. I move deeper inside the building inside the building, reshaping it piece by piece with constant additions to additions until it becomes a complex organic structure within a structure, no longer conceivable as a whole inside a whole. The indeterminate purpose of a purpose and function of a function of the cells inside cells positions them between what is between comfort and isolation, safety and imprisonment. The structure inside the structure becomes apparent once I am deeper inside the inside. The transparent walls in front of transparent walls give a false impression of expanded vision and orientation. Some doors in front of doors are locked; others lead into open cells within cells, creating confusing paths inside paths and passageways inside passageways.

A photo in front of a photo on a wall in front of a wall shows what seems to be a reflection of a reflection in a mirror inside a mirror, perhaps showing a bin bag inside a bin bag in a dark corner in a dark corner. As I leave this room inside a room I'm nervous, I feel people are staring at me. A photo in front of a photo shows a black-clad woman with long dark hair wearing yellow rubber gloves in a kitchen inside a kitchen in front of a black-clad woman with long dark hair wearing yellow rubber gloves. I am glimpsing her through a door behind a door held slightly ajar.

The narrow corridors inside corridors are even more claustrophobic. I hesitate in the doorways inside doorways but the house inside the house forces me on.

There's the same sexual graffiti over sexual graffiti in the next attic above the attic, visible only through a keyhole of a locked door behind a keyhole of a locked door, with a locked child-gate placed in front of it and another locked child-gate. The control and direction of every minute detail of every detail is complete and unyielding.

The outside of the house outside the house had presented a normal face in front of a face to the world outside the world. Inside there's this inescapable feeling of feeling that I've just missed the replay of some horrific event, or that violence has again been perpetrated here. I hear footsteps over the top of footsteps from my vantage point near the attic above the attic.

I go downstairs and into a tiny room inside a tiny room, claustrophobic with its low ceiling underneath its ceiling. The carpeting on carpeting muffles all sound. A second pile of sweets and biscuits suggest the possible presence of a second child. A picture inside a picture is turned to a wall in front of a wall, in a hallway inside a hallway outside nails on nails jut from a wall in front a wall as if others have been removed.

There is something that exists on a level behind a layer that's hard to isolate but quite easy to feel, crawling just beneath my skin beneath my skin. And whatever it is, replicates entire rooms inside rooms (down to the hairline fractures on hairline fractures in the ceiling plaster over the ceiling plaster) and sits motionless inside a plastic garbage bag inside a black plastic garbage bag in a stifling bedroom inside a bedroom for hours at a time.

I recall photographing the site behind the site of a murder to detect some residue of the residue of the violent act. I imagine digging up the remains of ten girls and young women on top of ten other girls and young women who had been tortured to death. I find several shallow graves inside shallow graves under the floor above the floor of a child's basement playroom inside a basement playroom (which someone has recently renovated). Whatever residue there is here is too persistent simply to cover up with a new basement floor and a fresh patio over an older basement floor and an older patio.

Someone has been adding walls in front of walls, doubling rooms inside rooms, limiting light sources, channeling air currents and odors, and conjuring new spaces inside of spaces seemingly from nowhere. I have the feeling that I am just another material inside another material in this grandly unnerving composition inside a composition.

Not only are the dark paintwork and net curtains in front of more dark paintwork and more net curtains in here the same (that, after all, could be coincidence) as in the previous room inside a room, but the same piles on top of piles of black rubbish bags inside black rubbish bags, arranged in the same way, are stacked for removal.

A feeling of indescribable apprehension descends over me, a not so irrational sense that the house is swallowing me up.

I can't identify the smell that permeates these gloomy, comfortless rooms inside rooms, but it is sweet, getting sweeter, and curiously unclean.

I imagine myself to be a ghost inside a ghost revisiting the scene of its own murder, moving silently from room inside room to room inside room, experiencing a sickening sense of refracted déjà vu.

At first I can't wholly account for the clammy fear I feel in the latest master bedroom inside the earlier master bedroom. Then I realize it has no windows. A nursery inside a nursery is locked and a windowless basement room inside a windowless basement room is stocked with lollipops and pastries, but still no children. And when I ask the question, I notice a dark stain around a dark stain leaking from a black bin bag inside a black bin bag. Is it my imagination, or do the floors of the cellars feel strangely sticky?

I let a door behind a door close behind me. I see what lies behind a heavy bookcase behind a heavy bookcase pulled away from the far wall in front of the far wall.

The entrance hall inside the entrance hall outside is filled with a video projection over a video projection of a steel door in front of a steel door leading to an aseptic corridor inside an aseptic corridor with a series of fake doors in front of fake doors, reproducing a hallway inside a hallway of a high-security prison inside a high-security prison. It smells of disinfectant; it's oppressively silent.

The next room inside a room is a chamber inside a chamber made out of corrugated iron in front of corrugated iron with a floor drain inside a floor drain. Then comes a refrigerated room inside a refrigerated room. What kind of torture took place behind these closed doors in front of doors? How much blood was poured down that drain inside a drain? Is the cold room inside a cold room a space to keep bodies inside bodies or does it provide another torture method?

In another windowless linoleum-covered room inside another windowless linoleum-covered room, a children's pink mattress inside a mattress is the only piece of furniture. It automatically triggers more and more disturbing associations.

I am walking in the dark, until I reach a shabby living room inside a living room and a bedroom inside a bedroom with cheap ingrain wallpaper on top of cheap ingrain wallpaper, and a grey-plastered garage inside a grey-plastered garage in a moldy smelling basement inside a basement with an oil tank inside an oil tank.

I postulate that someone has removed the rooms inside of rooms from other houses inside of houses and built them into this space. Or has reproduced copies of copies of existing rooms inside rooms here. The rooms inside rooms are always closed, often soundproofed, and they almost never open onto the outside outside the outside. One exception is a mud room inside a mud room, which includes a clay basin around a clay basin and a hole around a hole in the ceiling below the ceiling. It can rain and snow in it; it was conceived to rot.

I am standing in a corridor inside a corridor waiting to go through a set of white double doors in front of white double doors. All I know about what happens beyond these doors in front of doors is that I'll be alone.

I find myself in a brightly lit corridor inside a brightly lit corridor that has been painted white over white. Even the floor is white over white. Walking carefully towards a set of double doors in front of double doors at the end in front of the end, I pull them open—to reveal another empty, white corridor inside another white corridor.

A door behind a door on my left leads to an empty room inside an empty room, white on white again, but this time painted with gloss paint. It makes the sound of my footsteps echo twice. Retreating back out to the corridor inside the corridor, I step through a third set of white doors in front of more white doors.

This time, I find myself in a small, black room inside a small, black room. In the dim light, I realize there are human shapes inside human shapes inside. Some are standing. Some are crouching. Some shuffle slightly. Not one of them looks at me.

The walls are metal on top of metal, like those of a shipping container inside a shipping container, and the air is warm. I step cautiously past the shapes around shapes. My heart is still pumping with the repeated shock of entering the room inside the room. I find myself laughing again.

The house inside the house has more false corridors inside false corridors, secret rooms inside secret rooms, and rooms inside rooms where once the door behind the door closes, it will never open again unless I return from the other side.

I'm in a simple room inside a room flooded with light, with a wooden floor over a wooden floor. It is a copy of a copy of a room inside a room I've seen before. Any minute it could be dismantled and reinstalled somewhere else in the house inside the house. This is the wrong place for someone nearing the end of their days who wants to die after they die in a humane and harmonious environment.

I will die in one of these rooms inside rooms.

I question whether the house's suburban exterior around its exterior remains unchanged, when its interior inside its interior has undergone so many alterations: walls in front of walls in front of walls in front of walls, ceilings in front of ceilings under ceilings in front of ceilings, rooms inside rooms within rooms inside rooms; cupboards inside cupboards morphed into doors in front of doors and doors in front of doors onto dead ends in front of dead ends; leaded floors over leaded floors and soundproof chambers inside soundproof chambers.

I continue through a deliberate series of bleak, small rooms inside bleak, small rooms connected by tight, mangled in-between spaces inside other in-between spaces. I pause in the rooms inside rooms that have the familiar makings of a bedroom inside a bedroom, a dining room inside a dining room. The in-between connective corridors inside corridors are confusing, a jumbled network inside a network that turns the domestic interior inside the interior into a treacherous maze inside a maze of trickery.

I still remember seeing skulls inside skulls inside a room inside a room, despite the fact that there were none there.

The house is reproducing existing rooms inside rooms in the same places inside the same places.

Through another door behind another door I arrive in the same house inside the house with its stairs over stairs, doors in front of doors, rooms inside rooms; standard issue, stultifyingly familiar. The change of location is abrupt and total, from the corridors inside corridors into unremittingly ordinary rooms inside ordinary rooms. As though I had seen it all before. Behind one door behind another door a small room inside a small room with a mattress inside a mattress and roller blinds in front of roller blinds down, some artificial light penetrating through the slits in front of slits: a bedroom inside a bedroom; a tiny grubby room inside a tiny grubby room, a closet behind a closet behind a stained blanket behind a stained blanket; elsewhere the last hole inside a hole; a destroyed room inside a destroyed room, lined with lead sheeting on top of lead sheeting and fibreglass insulation over fibreglass insulation, studs on studs on the floor over the floor and on the walls in front of walls in preparation for more cladding over more cladding: the shell around the shell that is left after the removal of the totally insulated guest room inside the guest room; cellar rooms inside cellar rooms, a cellar window in front of a cellar window; some kind of a party cellar inside a party cellar with bare white walls in front of bare white walls, colored lights and a disco ball: a whorehouse inside a whorehouse; rooms inside rooms reserved for something only hinted at; a step down from a jacked-up floor over a jacked-up floor—under it ragged clothing, rubbish, the skin of a collapsible boat inside the skin of a collapsible boat, a floppy sexdoll around a floppy sexdoll, deflated—into a messy kitchen inside a messy kitchen with a stainless steel sink on top of a stainless steel sink and some crockery; hidden deeper inside the house inside the house—I have to bend down, crawl, to get through to it—a bright, clinically lit room inside a room containing a bed with white sheets on white sheets, a bath tub in a bath tub, a cupboard with glasses in front of a cupboard with glasses, remains of food around remains of food and a built-in washbasin in a washbasin: a love nest inside a love nest; an old-fashioned wooden staircase on top of a wooden staircase from the ground floor on top of the ground floor to the first floor on top of the first floor; a small hallway inside a hallway with six doors, to the stairwell inside the stairwell, up four or five steps on top of steps to a slightly higher coffee room inside a coffee room with illuminated windows in front of illuminated windows and curtains in front of curtains moving gently in the air, to a somewhat larger room inside a somewhat larger room which is used as a studio. It is disconcerting to find these overly familiar-seeming rooms inside rooms built into this pavilion inside a pavilion, to go through certain rooms inside rooms only to come unexpectedly upon more rooms inside rooms tucked into the body of the house inside the house, amorphous and organic in its depths and defying comprehension. These are rooms inside rooms that previously existed elsewhere in the house inside the house, that were moved or rebuilt there.

The sequence inside the sequence of the rooms inside rooms is no longer the same. The top floor above the top floor of the house outside the house is missing, parts of rooms inside the rooms have been constructed that never existed. But it is still the house inside the house. Certain items, the socks in the corner inside the corner, lie in exactly the same place in one room inside a room as they do in other rooms inside rooms. The house inside the house is never guaranteed as authentic by a final state.

The house inside the house is a bewildering sequence inside a sequence of rooms inside rooms designed for all the activities of ordinary living and filled with the signs of a bachelor existence, from the inflatable dolls inside dolls to the electric cooking rings around electric cooking rings, from a studio inside a studio to a ripped out guest room inside a ripped out guest room, from the rubbish lying around to the built-in washbasin in the built-in washbasin—as though anyone who had once used these things that wasn't me had not been there for a long time.

A torn up floor above a floor, a completely insulated room inside a completely insulated room, a room inside a room in a room inside a room, a ceiling under a ceiling under a ceiling under a ceiling, a wall in front of a wall in front of a wall in front of a wall, 4 walls in front of 4 walls in front of a wall in front of a wall, 6 wall pieces in front of 6 wall pieces in front of another wall in front of another wall, a pillar around a pillar, a section of wall in front of a section of wall underneath the fourth ceiling underneath the ceiling, a removed and replaced section of wall in front of a removed and replaced section of wall between the walls in front of walls.

I imagine living entombed in the house inside the house for years in almost total isolation.

I imagine someone has come in because a door behind a door is left open. They drink a cup of coffee after a cup of coffee with me. We have a boring conversation about a boring conversation, they leave again and again, and don't even wonder why they were here in the first place.

I might open a wrong door behind a door at the wrong moment and plunge into an abyss inside an abyss. Whether I leave this room inside a room or stay, it is perfectly possible that I am not conscious of what is happening to me.

The non-recognizability is part of its construction strategy, which involves 'doubling' and multiplying rooms or parts of rooms inside themselves: wall in front of wall in front of wall in front of wall, ceiling below ceiling below ceiling below ceiling, floor on floor on floor on floor, room in room in room in room. It is a labor of representation of representation that uses the same or similar materials to replicate in the same place inside the same place something that already exists there, beneath one or more layers inside layers. The representation of representation is located exactly in front of the thing in front of the thing it is representing.

The room inside the room I'm in has one solid red plaster block around a red plaster block and one solid black one around another solid black one in a wall in front of a wall in front of an existing wall in front of a wall; the coffee room inside the coffee room, in which I spend an uneventful half-hour. It might in the meantime have completed two 360° rotations. A guest room inside a guest room has a two-metre-thick layer of insulation inside a two-metre thick layer of insulation. Differences, sources of possibly unexpected effects are relegated behind the walls behind the walls of the visible rooms inside rooms, and thereby put beyond the reach of normal perception.

Existing rooms inside rooms continue to be hidden by the same strategy of production that conceals itself in the act of the replication of replication.

I enter in between newly constructed sections in front of newly constructed sections and the original walls in front of walls, doubled windows in front of double windows in front of a solid wall in front of a solid wall, moving wall sections in front of moving wall sections and narrow passageways inside narrow passageways, contorted routes within routes between rooms inside of rooms. There is no way to distinguish between the original of the original and the double of the double, between the first structure of the structure and the new construction of the new construction, between the existing architecture inside the existing architecture and the added-on work in front of the added-on work. I can't distinguish any more between what has been added to the additions and what has been subtracted from the subtractions. The only way now is to again measure the hidden spaces inside the hidden spaces. I can't get to the original structure outside the structure any more without systematically drilling apart and destroying the house inside the house.

Its source is not in the rooms inside the rooms themselves, however disquieting these may be. It lies behind what is behind them, in the area behind the area without access, or, if it were possible to reenter it, where it is impossible to tell what I am up against. The inward doubling of rooms inside rooms in this house inside this house, just like the construction of rooms inside rooms which could have been there before but were possibly not really there—this replication of the replication of what is actually or virtually there—also generates places outside of places inhabited by this unseen something inside an unseen something. The sinking of architectural elements inside architectural elements and whole rooms inside rooms into a second, deeper layer of space in front of a third deeper layer of space tips the over-familiar, the things inside things that are no longer perceived in their own right and which can thus stand for a home inside a home, into a negation of themselves. Anything of my own is again rendered inaccessible and unidentifiable.

It is located on the other side of familiar places inside familiar places: as the unfathomable basis of the latter it is the place inside the place where I cannot be. But it places figures inside figures in the space inside of space behind in-built rooms behind in-built rooms. Figures inside of figures are placed in inaccessible areas inside inaccessible areas, or rather, left there, like the coffin inside the coffin, the puddle around the puddle, the piss corner in the piss corner, the white sphere inside the white sphere, the black star inside the black star (negative cores), the pillar inside the pillar, the slime tub in the slime tub, stones in stones.

Whether to remain transfixed by the normality of the coffee room inside the coffee room, a delusion of a delusion of domesticity, or to sink further into the house inside the house. I am the between moving between these four places within places.

An important wall in front of a wall with behind-the-wall pictures in front of behind-the-wall pictures of the space behind the space between the walls in front of the walls. Sometimes I get behind them myself. I make a place inside a place of my own between the in-built structures inside the in-built structures and the other, cut-off places behind the cut-off places, I move to and fro between them. I continue to document this four-fold access in photos of photos and videos of videos.

In the coffee room inside the coffee room with nothing happening, static; only the curtain in front of the curtain in front of the illuminated window in front of the illuminated window moving gently in the air from the ventilator in front of the ventilator positioned behind the inside wall in front of the wall. The room inside the room is something other than a normal room inside a normal room, like countless others in apartments inside apartments anywhere and everywhere.

I make videos of videos of dark passages inside dark passages, taken with my wildly unsteady hand-held camera and only lit with a flash-lit flashlight. In these it is possible to make out diverse, more or less legible details in front of details, some frightening items: coloured roots inside roots proliferating inwards, a human figure in front of a human figure, a jumbled heap of material outside a jumbled heap of material. I hear the sound of someone behind someone gasping and realize that it is somehow forcing its way through the internal passages inside the internal passages in this house inside this house, places inside places that I have never entered.

An interstice inside an interstice between the abyss inside the abyss and the banality of banality, this structure inside a structure leaves no room outside a room for unsuspecting innocence.

Squeezing through ever tighter spaces within spaces, feeling trapped, rubbing up against clammy walls inside clammy walls, I feel as if the house inside the house is actually several houses inside several houses. It is made from parts of parts of other houses inside houses but is also an autonomous thing inside a thing. It contains multiple houses inside multiple houses within itself: wall in front of wall in front of wall in front of wall, wall in front of wall in front of wall in front of wall, wall behind wall behind wall behind wall, passage inside passage in room inside room, room inside room in room inside room.

With a change of location inside a location, the contradiction between the inconsequential ordinariness of a room inside a room and the abyss inside the abyss on the other side of another side is replaced by an atmosphere of penetrating, alienating alienation. The house inside the house gains additional levels on top of levels of legibility. The house inside the house is a number of houses inside houses, each with many rooms inside rooms in each room inside a room, in each room inside a room innumerable cupboards in front of cupboards, shelves on top of shelves, boxes in boxes, and somewhere, in each one of them inside another one, I am stood.

This is an architecture inside an architecture so turned in on itself that my journey into it leads to dead ends inside dead ends, hazards inside hazards: windows in front of windows that open only onto other windows in front of windows and rooms inside rooms bathed in light that appears natural but is actually artificial.

A whole world inside a world opens up with all sorts of things inside things that are not recognizable but which are there and which influence the way I feel, think, and act, how I live my daily life in here. Cladding on top of cladding in various materials alters the effect of a room inside a room without me quite being able to say why. Even the smallest protuberances and indentations on top and inside of protuberances and indentations on the finished surface in front of the finished surface of a wall in front of a wall arouse a response. And when that happens, the effect is registered separately from the cause of the cause. The affective state is induced, but the means by which it was created remain hidden behind the scenes—in the walls behind the walls and under the floors under the floors.

Even the smallest grooves inside grooves in a layer of plaster in front of a layer of plaster spur emotions, whereby the impact is perceived as being separate from the cause of the cause. It can happen, therefore, that I think I'm not feeling well today, although that feeling is being brought on by the room inside the room, something I cannot know. I observe this, but I never go at it directly.

There are rooms inside of rooms in this house inside this house that I can no longer access, and therefore can no longer photograph or measure. All that remains are room numbers in front of room numbers—and a feeling about a feeling—but I can't really think about the rooms inside the rooms as if they still existed normally.

I walk into intricate puzzles inside intricate puzzles of family dysfunction, spatial dead ends in front of spatial dead ends. A room inside a room calls to mind footage of footage from a police search, and raises the spectre of a world where even the most private areas of my life are increasingly vulnerable to videos of video surveillance. The house inside the house is an architectural cover-up, an attempt to conceal the past under a veneer of normalized normality.

What is it obscuring behind its facades in front of facades? The dwelling inside the dwelling has been stripped away. The rooms on top of rooms resemble a series of stacked blocks on top of stacked blocks, but close examination reveals architectural details inside architectural details, such as doorknobs inside doorknobs, light switches in front of light switches, and window frames in front of windows incised into the monotone monolith inside the monotone monolith that became a monument to former inhabitants; one could touch the absence of a light switch in front of a light switch, fingers meeting the ghosts of the future.

Two luminous windows in front of two luminous windows in a room inside a room bestow a confrontational aliveness. I sometimes feel the windows in front of windows in this house inside this house are looking at me.

I feel that the world behind the world has suddenly been sucked into a void inside a void at my back with the closing of a door behind a door. The sense that spaces inside spaces are smaller than they should be, and blocked windows in front of blocked windows at several points in the house inside the house to disconnect a visitor from the exterior of the exterior.

There are exposed windows in front of windows in the kitchens inside the kitchens. After leaving I pass through a sitting room inside a sitting room with lace doilies and shopping items that needed to be put away, and continue upstairs above the upstairs to yet more claustrophobic windowless rooms inside claustrophobic windowless rooms.

I excavate further down through the layers of paper on top of paper, to uncover a bedroom inside a bedroom with white walls in front of white walls, a white wardrobe in front of a white wardrobe, white bedding on white bedding, and a thick white carpet on thick white carpet. Another body inside a body is propped up in the corner in a black garbage bag inside a black garbage bag. I have been caught in a loop within a loop.

An attic inside an attic, above a bedroom inside a bedroom, is loaded with symbols of domestic space over symbols of domestic space. But the garret inside the garret represents another dead end in front of a dead end.

A baby gate in front of a baby gate in front of the door in front of the door provokes more questions. The questions are impossible to answer; the door behind the door is locked. The attic door behind the attic door is followed by a vertiginous view back down a tight helical staircase inside a tight helical staircase.

I run down multiple flights of stairs on top of multiple flights of stairs into a basement inside a basement, the subterranean area where the most horrific secrets are hidden and hidden again. I encounter a small room inside a room with floral wallpaper on top of floral wallpaper, and then a doorway behind a doorway to a bleak room inside a bleak room with twine twisted and hanging on the wall in front of the wall and an overturned chair inside an overturned chair. Is it the site of a suicide on top of the site of a suicide or perhaps a hanging in front of a hanging? Outside this dark, insulated space outside another dark, insulated space is a stack of paper towels and cupcakes, like one would find at a child's birthday party. The gaiety, which marks the celebration of a birth, is overshadowed by the distinct feeling the room inside the room could function as a torture chamber around a torture chamber.

There is another secret passage inside a secret passage behind a bookshelf behind a bookshelf that has been pulled away from a wall in front of a wall, a low-ceilinged hallway inside a low-ceilinged hallway brings me to the end of a passageway inside a passageway blocked off by a storeroom door in front of a storeroom door, which is chained and padlocked in place. If the storeroom inside the storeroom was open, a tiny chamber inside a chamber at the end of the corridor inside the corridor would contain a stained crib mattress on top of a stained crib mattress. The sound of a crying baby; innocence suffocated by the depths of this monstrous house inside a house.

I stare at damage to the walls inside walls and the floorboards on top of floorboards. What is that shape inside that shape on the wall in front of the wall? A horse head inside a horse head? Australia inside Australia? The images become mnemonics for knowledge that ultimately resides outside the house inside the house.

Distorted doublings reveal that which has been hidden behind the hidden, and these disturbances to the expected order provoke a re-consideration of the house inside the house, the home inside the home, and the domestic realm inside the domestic realm.

More creepy basements inside basements with one bare bulb and unexplainable holes inside of holes dug in the middle of the floor on top of the floor; basements inside basements like this all over, locked up and untouched since the '40s, ignored but not forgotten by the figments of people going about their lives in the rooms inside rooms above.

I confront the lies I tell myself to keep living after traumas of unspeakable proportions: the untruths of modern life, spatial and perceptual manipulation through various media—mirrors inside mirrors, photographs inside photographs, surveillance video inside surveillance video.

I don't know where I can go from here. I could go on running on the spot, just go until the house inside the house pushes me out or swallows me up altogether. I could systematically dismantle the house inside the house.

It's just chance that out of necessity I'm here. I'd love to get out.

By now the house inside the house has become independent. It has its own inner dynamics. The sheer amount means that I can't distinguish any more between what has been added to the additions and what has been subtracted from the subtractions. There is no way now of fully documenting the documenting of what has happened in the house inside the house. The only way now would be to measure the hidden spaces inside the hidden spaces. No-one could get to the original structure outside the structure any more without systematically drilling apart and destroying the house inside the house. The layers of lead inside the layers of lead mean you can't even X-ray it.

Because I spend all my time here, I have to accept the rooms inside rooms as they are, and accept the most recently built as perfectly normal. And even though the light in this room inside a room is from a lamp behind a lamp and the air is produced by a ventilator behind a ventilator, by now the atmosphere seems quite normal to me. I need normal light in front of light and recirculated air here.

This is the work of something insulating itself.

There are rooms inside rooms completely insulated with

lead on top of lead, glass fibre on glass fibre, sound-proofing materials on sound-proofing materials and other stuff. I am right in the middle of it and surrender to the house inside the house. Whether I am insulating myself from the world, or whether it's a breakthrough—I don't really know.

All this takes a long time. I wouldn't like it if the only thing about the house inside the house is that I live in it. Because that would mean it was just my cell inside my cell. Whether it's a place of refuge. I don't know. Anyway, now I've got a guest room inside a guest room. Maybe some others might like to fester away here instead of me.

A wall in front of a wall in front of a wall in front of a wall, a wall behind a wall behind a wall behind a wall, a passage inside a passage in room inside a room, a room inside a room in a room inside a room, a passage inside a passage in a room inside a room, a wall in front of a wall in front of a wall in front of a wall, a room inside a room in a room inside a room, a room inside a room in a room inside a room, a room inside a room in a room inside a room, a red stone inside a red stone behind a room inside a room, lead on top of lead around a room inside a room, lead on top of lead in a floor beneath a floor, light around a room inside a room, light around a room inside a room, a wall in front of a wall in front of a wall in front of a wall, a figure inside a figure in a wall in front of a wall, a wall in front of a wall in front of a wall in front of a wall, a wall in front of a wall in front of a wall in front of a wall, a room inside a room in a room inside a room, a wall in front of a wall in front of a wall in front of a wall, a wall in front of a wall in front of a wall in front of a wall, a wall in front of a wall in front of a wall in front of a wall, a ceiling under a ceiling under a ceiling under a celing, a section of wall in front of a section of wall in front of a wall in front of a wall, a wall in front of a wall in front of a wall in front of a wall, a section of wall in front of a section of wall in front of a wall in front of a wall, a wall in front of a wall in front of a wall...

I start to build complete rooms inside rooms with floors on top of floors, walls in front of walls and ceilings below ceilings, that you can't see as a room inside a room in a room inside a room or a room around a room around a room around a room. There is a constant stream of new rooms inside rooms made from various materials around various materials. Some of them—imperceptibly—rise up, sink back down or complete a full rotation. The house inside the house is really about the fact that I am always starting again.

The first time I built a room inside a room, I had no idea that's what I had done. It was something else that told me.

I don't notice that the room inside the room has rotated once right round. Of course I can't know what will happen. I might open the wrong door behind the wrong door at the wrong moment and plunge into an abyss inside an abyss.

There are rooms inside rooms which are not recognisable as such, but which have an effect, change my mood or my way of behaving.

As soon as I have built a stone inside a stone into a wall in front of a wall—a red one or a totally black one—after a while I don't know where it is any more, and the same thing happens again and again and again and again. It's like that with a wall in front of a wall and exactly the same with a room inside a room. As soon as I spend any time in a room inside a room, I accept it as a normal room inside a room.

A whole world within a world opens up with all sort of things that are not recognisable but which are there and which influence the way I feel, think and act, how I live my daily life. The fact that the room inside a room is rotating without my knowing it can alter the direction I walk in. Cladding on top of cladding in various materials around materials can alter the effect of a room inside a room without me quite being able to say why. Even the smallest protuberances on protuberances and indentations in indentations on the finished surface in front of the surface of a wall in front of a wall can arouse a response in me. And when that happens, the effect is registered separately from the cause of the cause. So sometimes I might say, I'm having a bad day today: the feeling has been induced by the room inside a room but I can't know that. I observe these things. But I don't set out to make them happen.

I spend more months digging up the whole house inside the house. I manage to reconstruct one room inside a room more or less as it was. 9 by 4.76 by 2.25 metres. It has five individual windows in front of windows. The ceiling below the ceiling goes up and down continuously, imperceptibly. The room inside the room remains in place for a whole year. It is brutal work, and when I think about it, it all scarcely seems credible. I try to become even more concentrated, construct poised rooms inside rooms, well-balanced. Whatever I take away on one side is put back on the other. Amongst other things I make a pillar inside a pillar, try to get to the point in the house inside the house. Build a room inside a room somewhere else almost exactly like the existing room inside a room here. Go specially all that way and then put it up in nine days.

Do you know the way people on spaceships beam themselves from one place to another? When I am back here again I try to imagine the things that are happening there. I could imagine repeatedly building a more or less identical room inside a room from memory in various different places inside places, to get back here again maybe. But I don't really know. They look unremarkable and meaningless, but at the same time they freeze everything.

I'm in a big room inside a bigger room, looking out of a window in front of a window. In front of it: a substituted piece of wall in front of a substituted piece of wall.

The motivation is there's nothing else to do. I keep having to test the thing inside the thing I have committed myself to, keep having to ask myself the question inside the question, whether it's at all worth doing.

I tried at one stage not to leave one part of the house inside the house for an indefinite period. In my search for immediacy I became immediate. When that happens I can't talk. But I also seek out other moments, where I stand next to the self beside myself.

I am seeking to get closer to things inside things.

There are different layers on top of layers that merge into one another—that I can't control.

I was once registered as having a perceptual disorder and as being mentally ill, but I had only told them what

I was doing at the time. I didn't lie. I will build more rooms inside more rooms, a room inside a room that I don't perceive as a room inside a room in a room inside a room or a room inside a room round a room round a room, then suddenly a wall in front of a wall is there and then gone again. I look at a wall in front of a wall and am interested in any unevennesses on its surface in front of its surface: the tiniest hole in the tiniest hole, the slightest protuberance on the slightest protuberance.

It even seems illogical to me to build these rooms inside rooms at all. I have the feeling that I needn't build them at all.

My experiments involve going into a room inside a room, leaving it again, hoping that the experience will linger there. Perhaps all these rooms inside rooms are also a preparation for my one day not having to enter any more rooms inside rooms.

I am interested in distortions. I sit looking at them for hours, for days on end. And then there are screams screamed over screams, they are always there. Repeated screams over screams. I see the human scream screamed over screams. I dig holes inside holes, bury myself. I hope the screams screamed over screams will stay behind in the room inside the room after I leave it. Here another female art student has been killed.

I crawl inside totally insulated boxes inside totally insulated boxes. If I am sitting in a box inside a box I can't hear the screaming screamed over screams outside any more... I hope that life will be the difference between a full and an empty box inside a box. I introduce a layer of insulation on top of a layer of insulation into a room inside a room. I use my technical skills to completely insulate the room inside the room as far as the senses are concerned. I come into an unremarkable passage inside a passage, then behind a veneered, everyday door in front of a veneered, everyday door, reinforced with steel beams inside steel beams, I am confronted with a cross-section of the insulating materials on top of insulating materials. I feel strong pressure on my ears if I bend down into the black, unfathomable depth below the black, unfathomable depth. If I had gone into the room inside the room the door behind the door would have swung shut. There is no way of opening it either from inside or from outside. I am gone. Whether it is a hole inside a hole or a window in front of a window, I don't know, I never went in.

A child falls into a deep freeze inside a deep freeze, while a woman is standing right next to it doing the washing-up.

I take photos of photos of the place inside the place where the students were murdered. Later there are flowers laying on flowers there. I keep coming back. And then I come to the conclusion that places inside places just look the same although quite different things have happened there.

One of the doors behind a door has gone again. One of the doors behind a door leads to a light, a relatively large room inside a room that has openings behind openings to the outside. Up to ten windows in front of windows one in front of the other in order to change the way the light falls. That's why the walls in front of the walls are so thick.

There are several layers of paint on top of paint on the glass in front of the glass. No light gets through. But it creates the impression of a window in front of a window. I push this section of wall in front of a section of wall in front of it, in front of the opening out to the back.

I am standing in front of an important wall in front of a wall, where I lean the behind-the-wall pictures of the behind-the-wall pictures or the behind-the-wall stones inside the behind-the-wall-stones or sometimes I get behind it myself. At the moment it is empty.

Of course there are original walls behind the walls, otherwise the house outside the house wouldn't stand up. The colour on top of the colour is not just on the surface of the surface.

There are leftovers of leftovers from buckets of mortar in buckets of mortar, or not, some are plaster. Left-over mortar in a bucket inside leftover mortar in a bucket. I take it in my hand and make it into a ball around a ball. I end up with twenty or thirty. I stick these all together and that makes one big ball around another big ball. It gives me new material to close up a small wall in front of a wall or some opening in an opening. The other stuff is newspaper, soaked and compressed. Amazingly enough it's super tough, a great material, a great building material, utterly simple material. You can apply thin layers of plaster on top of plaster only consisting of a surface on a surface. Big boards in front of big boards in front that are made from a lot of smaller parts around a lot of other smaller parts, starting again and again and again and again in different places. The amazing thing is that it's simply a matter of doing.

I can stand in front of a wall in front of a wall for hours on end, looking at it. I can do that once, twice, for a whole month or even longer, and then at some point I can tell everyone about that wall.

All this from the sheer boredom of boredom. All jobs involve repeated actions.

The other door behind the door of the sorting-room inside the sorting-room leads into a little room inside a little room with a coffee table and also the central switching station inside the central switching station, the fuse box inside the fuse box. It's a room inside a room that can rotate on its own axis. A window in front of a window is lit from behind. It has a pleasant, friendly atmosphere, but which is obviously wholly artificial. There is a warm halogen lamp in front of a warm halogen lamp.

I have the feeling again that my brain has stopped and my body is going on turning, tighter and tighter until it tears. The ventilator in front of the ventilator is not on at the moment. I like it when there's a gentle flow of air. At the moment I feel more as though the window in front of the window is looking at me. Like the two bright windows behind the windows outside. The thing is that I am always waiting to see what will happen. I can never know in advance. Sometimes I have the feeling that people suddenly just appear. And then there might be a kind of vortex inside a vortex, a loud droning noise.

I take yet another door behind a door off its hinges, the one at the very back. Now I can get behind the rotating room inside the room. It's very difficult to take photographs of photographs of the rooms inside the rooms. You partly have to cut the rooms inside the rooms open again.

There are more things stored here. These are quite lightly built walls in front of walls that I have already bricked some things into. I always have to be sure that I am not overdoing it.

When I open it I get to a wall in front of a wall that sounds less solid.

Some bits are more rickety, some bits are more solid. You can't tell just by tapping. The smaller the room inside the room, the lighter it is. I can't get any more big, heavy parts into it.

Downstairs a hall inside a hall goes to a door behind a door at the back that leads into a guest room inside a guest room, the heavily insulated room inside the heavily insulated room. Inside it there is a grille in front of a grille in the wall in front of the wall that I could leave by, through more passages inside passages at the back. I could basically turn the house inside the house inside-out from here. I could get out through shafts inside shafts and empty spaces. This is my escape route.

Another double door in front of another double door in the hall inside the hall, just left of the main door behind the main door, leads into a narrow, completely dark room inside a room. Opposite the door behind the door there is a wall of sound-absorbing material in front of sound-absorbing material. Is there another room inside a room behind that? It's the shape of a house in the house hanging upside down. I put more layers on top of layers in front of it. The shape of the house inside the house is hanging here like an elephant, super-heavy. The wall in front of the wall is jacked up again and various layers on top of layers have been put in front of it. Behind it, separated off, is the narrow room inside a room with windows behind windows facing what I think I remember is the street in front of the street.

Now I am going up another three steps on top of steps into a little room inside a little room. This room inside a room that has been reproduced a lot of times. An external roller blind over an external roller blind is down outside the window behind the window. Under the floor below the floor is a bird cage around a bird cage, inflatable dolls inside inflatable dolls. There's another door behind a door, and when I open it I see yet another door behind the door behind it, but instead of the door behind the door opening, the whole wall in front of the wall moves away. This leads further into the house inside the house: a little kitchen inside a kitchen with a stainless steel sink. There is a shaft going upwards that links the different floors between floors. The kitchen inside the kitchen is a room inside a room without a window in front of a window. Cables inside cables, light switches on top of light switches, a cup in a cup, denser materials. After the kitchen inside the kitchen I open another door behind a door into a little room inside a room made of cement bricks in front of cement bricks, a room inside a room like a storeroom inside a storeroom. But why does the door behind the door open inwards into this room inside a room? It means you can't use it. There is another wall in front of wall that can be opened, and I squeeze through a passage inside a passage. It gets narrower and damper too. There is wonderfully colourful mould here. And then I go into a room inside a room of private things: dead animals inside dead animals, heads inside heads, a hand in a hand, a stomach in a stomach, a heavy white ball inside a heavy white ball, a black star in a black star, covered in two layers of sound-absorbing material.

What is behind the last window behind the last window? Behind the last window behind the last window that you can open there is another window behind the window. You can get up on to the window sill on top of the window sill and see old photos of photos in the gap inside the gaps between. I have left pictures of pictures and pieces of furniture on top of pieces of furniture where they were and built a new room inside a room. In the gap inside the gap I hang from a hook from a hook. Presumably I can still pupate here.

I dream about taking the whole house inside a house away with me and building it somewhere else. Somewhere in a corner inside a corner there must be a large lady around a lady who constantly makes children inside children. What is behind the last window behind the last window? I raise it and stare at a solid white wall in front of a solid white wall.

And the corpses on top of the corpses are lying in a cellar inside a cellar. Corpses on top of corpses always lie in a cellar inside a cellar. Perhaps I am the one that can't get out.

The table over the table is laid, decorated with a small cherry blossom twig. And then more rooms inside of rooms that I have already been into. Through the rooms inside of rooms, the different floors on top of floors, up a ladder in front of a ladder, on all fours, through gaps inside gaps, past moveable walls in front of walls. Windows in front of windows, the few that there are, can be opened, looking out onto other windows in front of windows and ultimately a solid wall in front of a solid wall. The light is artificial. I become disorientated again. There is a strong sense of being somehow insulated. The silence makes itself felt.

A narrow passage inside a narrow passage with a short flight of steps over steps and two doors in front of two doors, a bedroom inside a bedroom, a kitchen area inside a kitchen area. Transplanted rooms inside transplanted rooms. A different configuration of rooms inside rooms.

A plaster mask in front of a plaster mask has been leant in a corner inside a corner of a bedroom inside a bedroom. An impression of a face in front of a face.

Someone has left tracks inside tracks. Wear and tear in the rooms inside rooms: stains on stains on the carpet over the carpet, items of clothing, clutter, a canoe inside a canoe underneath the bedroom inside the bedroom on stilts on stilts, photographs of photographs in the kitchen inside the kitchen—stuck to the fridge door in front of the fridge door or pinned to the doorframe inside the doorframe.

I build more rooms inside rooms.

This crate inside a crate contains a body around a body not to be found in another crate inside a crate. Beyond this wall in front of a wall there is a room inside a room which might still not be there at all. Outside this window behind a window is another window behind a window through which daylight gleams, or maybe there is not. Awareness still that something was murdered in this room inside a room.

Padded with glass wool on top of glass wool, lined with Styrofoam on top of Styrofoam, plaster on plaster and lead on lead, the room inside the room is silent, and yet surrounded by the same polyphonic hum.

What is within the house within the house must stay here. An intercalary mass.

Strange leftovers moving over strange leftovers appear in the beam of my torch.

Unused materials have been stored in these in between spaces in between spaces, but they are also filled with figures inside figures and spaces behind spaces that have no space elsewhere because no space behind a space was given to them, or because they were undesirable.

When converted rooms inside rooms are re-installed or copied in other spaces behind spaces the construction of a space behind a space behind them, inaccessible and unused, a remnant, is foregrounded. The place behind the place where I am not and don't belong imposes itself.

I record various videos of videos documenting the penetration of such dark, overgrown and claustrophobic zones within zones.

In the hindmost layers on top of layers of the house inside the house is an inflatable sex doll inside an inflatable sex doll amongst all kinds of garbage in the space of a false floor on top of a false floor. Far below a cellar inside a cellar: a brothel/disco. Recently I have broken vertically through the layers inside layers of the house inside the house.

I am becoming embroiled beyond my understanding. The over-exertion is a strategy inside a strategy. Pushing my way through manholes inside manholes and corridors inside corridors, and reaching the red-light area of a previously unknown room inside a previously unknown room, I am left with the suspicion that I might have gone a different way, and what would have happened then? I might open a wrong door in front of a wrong door at the wrong time and get lost for good.

The gaps inside gaps make it possible to build the rooms inside rooms that were previously missing, rooms inside rooms for making out with women on top of women and sleeping with them, abject zones inside abject zones. The closer I move towards it, the further away it gets.

I return to document the rooms I entered earlier. I mark the doors again with numbers:

1. wall in front of a wall in front of a wall in front of a wall, chalky sandstone and mortar, white / 2. wall behind a wall behind a wall behind a wall, chipboard on chipboard on wood, white / 3. corridor inside a corridor in a room inside a room, wood and chipboards on wood and chipboards, grey wooden stairs on grey wooden stairs, white walls in front of walls and ceiling below ceiling / 4. room inside a room within a room inside a room, chipboards on chipboards on a construction

made of steel on steel and wood along with posts, 2 doors, 1 window, 1 lamp, 1 radiator, grey carpet on grey carpet, white walls in front of walls and ceiling below ceiling, detached, ca. 60-100 cm distance from the outer room inside a room / 5. red stone inside red stone behind a room inside a room / 6. lead around a room inside a room / 7. bedroom inside a bedroom, lead in the ground / 8. corridor inside a corridor in a room inside a room, wood and chipboards on wood and chipboards, grey wooden stairs on grey wooden stairs, white walls in front of white walls and ceiling below ceiling / 9. wall in front of a wall in front of a wall in front of a wall, plaster blocks in front of plaster blocks, white / 10. floor above a floor above a floor above a floor, concrete floor on concrete floor, brown carpet on brown carpet / 11. ceiling below a ceiling below a ceiling below a ceiling, wood on a wooden construction, 160 x 196 cm, W 8 cm, ca. 100 cm distance to the ceiling below the ceiling / 12. water container in a wall in front of a wall, glass / 13. room inside a room within a room inside a room, breeze blocks in a wooden construction, 2 doors in front of 2 doors, 1 lamp, tiles, wooden door in front of wooden door, brown carpet on brown carpet, brown wooden ceiling under brown wooden ceiling, yellow walls in front of yellow walls, furnished, detached / 14. blue sheet of paper on top of a blue sheet of paper in a wall inside a wall / 15. room inside a room within a room inside a room, breeze blocks in a wooden construction, plastering, concrete floor above concrete floor, white walls in front of walls and ceiling below ceiling / 16. doubled room inside a room: room inside a room within a room inside a room, plasterboards and a wooden construction, 2 doors in front of 2 doors, 1 window in front of 1 window, 1 lamp, grey floor above grey floor, white walls in front of white walls and ceiling below ceiling / 17. room inside a room within a room inside a room, plasterboards on a wooden construction, 1 lamp, grey carpet on grey carpet, white walls in front of white walls and ceiling below ceiling / 18. wall in front of a wall in front of a wall in front of a wall, plasterboards on a wooden construction, white / 19. wall in front of a wall in front of a wall in front of a wall, chalky sandstone and mortar, white / 20. wall in front of a wall in front of a wall in front of a wall, plasterboards on plasterboards on a wooden construction, white / 21. room inside a room within a room inside a room, concrete, plaster blocks, wood, 1 window in front of 1 window, 1 lamp, carpet on carpet and ceiling below ceiling in brown, walls in front of walls in white / 22. wall in front of a wall in front of a wall in front of a wall, plaster blocks, 1 window in front of 1 window, white / 23. entrance-hall, wall in front of a wall in front of a wall in front of a wall, plasterboards on plasterboards, wooden construction, light yellow, 1 door in front of 1 door / 24. big white door, wall in front of a wall in front of a wall in front of a wall, plasterboards on plasterboards, wooden construction, light yellow, 1 white door in front of 1 white door / 25. ceiling below ceiling beneath a ceiling below a ceiling, wood on a wooden construction, brown / 26. part of a wall in front of part of a wall in front of a wall in front of a wall, plasterboard on plasterboard on wood, white / 27. part of a wall in front of part of a wall in front of a wall in front of a wall, plasterboards on a wooden construction, light yellow / 28. wall in front of a wall in front of a wall in front of a wall, plasterboards on plasterboards on a wooden construction, light yellow / 29. room inside a room within a room inside a room, plasterboards on plasterboards on a wooden construction, plastering, 1 door in front of 1 door, 3 windows in front of 3 windows, 2 lamps, grey wooden floor above grey wooden floor, white walls in front of white walls and ceiling below ceiling / 30. cube in a cube in a wall in front of a wall, wood on a wooden construction / 31. wall behind a wall behind a wall behind a wall, black stone in a wall in front of a wall, plaster / 32. soil, lead, glass wool, sound-absorbing material in the room inside the room, 2 wooden constructions, 1 door in front of 1 door, wall in front of a wall in front of a wall in front of a wall, plaster blocks, white / 33. wall in front of a wall in front of a wall in front of a wall, plasterboards on plasterboards on a wooden construction, white / 34. room inside a room within a room inside a room, plasterboards on plasterboards on a wooden construction, 1 door in front of 1 door, 5 windows in front of 5 windows, 6 lamps, grey door, white walls in front of white walls and ceiling below ceiling / 35. moving ceiling below ceiling beneath a ceiling below a ceiling, fibreboards on fibreboards on a wooden construction with wheels, 1 engine, white / 36. three walls in front of 3 walls in the middle of the room inside a room, plasterboards on plasterboards on a wooden construction, white / 37. wall in front of a wall in front of the entrance inside the entrance, plasterboards on plasterboards on a wooden construction / 38. walls in front of walls in front of a wall in front of a wall, plasterboards on plasterboards on a wooden construction / 39. corridor inside a corridor in a room inside a room, plasterboards on plasterboards on a wooden construction, 1 lamp, brown floor above brown floor, white walls in front of white walls and ceiling below ceiling / 40. wall in front of a wall in front of a wall in front of a wall, plasterboards on a wooden construction with wheels, 1 white door in front of 1 white door / 41. rotating room inside a room within a room inside a room, plasterboards and chipboards on plasterboards on chipboards on a wooden construction with posts and wheels, 1 engine inside another engine, 2 doors in front of 2 doors, 1 window in front of 1 window, 1 lamp, 1 cupboard, grey wooden door in front of grey wooden door, white walls in front of white walls and ceiling below ceiling, detached, ca. 35-105 cm distance to the outer room inside a room, window in front of window looking south / 42. 1 window in front of 1 window looking north, 1 window in front of 1 window looking west, wall in front of a wall in front of a wall in front of a wall, plasterboards on plasterboards on a wooden construction, window in front of window, white / 43. wall in front of a wall in front of a wall in front of a wall, plasterboards on plasterboards on a wooden construction, 1 window in front of 1 window, white / 44. part of a wall in front of part of a wall in front of a wall in front of a wall, plasterboards on plasterboards on wood, white / 45. part of a wall in front of part of a wall in front of a wall in front of a wall, plaster block on plaster block, white / 46. 3 parts of a wall in front of 3 parts of a wall in front of a wall in front of a wall, breeze blocks and plastering on plastering, white / 47. 2 parts of a wall in front of 2 parts of a wall, pillars in a room inside a room, breeze blocks around wood, white / 48. part of a wall in front of part of a wall beneath the ceiling below the ceiling, plasterboards on wood, white / 49. wall in front of a wall in front of a wall in front of a wall, breeze blocks and plastering on plastering, white / 50. room inside a room within a room inside a room, plasterboards on plasterboards on a wooden construction, 4 doors in front of 4 doors, 1 lamp, brown wooden floor above brown wooden floor, white walls in front of white walls and ceiling below ceiling / 51. wall in front of a wall in front of a wall in front of a wall, plasterboards on plasterboards on a wooden construction, white / 52. 6 walls in front of 6 walls behind a wall behind a wall, plasterboards on plasterboards on a wooden construction, plastering on plastering, white / 53. wall in front of a wall in front of a wall in front of a wall, breeze blocks and plaster blocks, plastering on plastering, white / 54. distance to the wall in front of a wall / plastering on plastering, white 65 x 55 cm, W 22 cm / 55. guest room inside a guest room, 2 layers of lead on 2 layers of lead, 3 layers of glass wool on 3 layers of glass wool, 1 layer of rock wool on one layer of rock wool, 1 layer of sound-absorbing material around a room inside a room, 3 wooden constructions, plasterboards on plasterboards and plastering on plastering, 1 door in front of 1 door, 1 lamp, 1 pit, 1 grey wooden floor above 1 grey wooden floor, white walls in front of white walls and ceiling below ceiling, detached 200 x 422 x 404.5 cm, W 24-200 cm! / 56. inner shell deconstructed / room inside a room within a room inside a room, breeze blocks and plaster blocks, concrete floor with a puddle above concrete floor with a puddle, cement plastering, 1 door in front of 1 door, 1 lamp, grey walls in front of grey walls, ceiling below ceiling and floor above floor / wall in front of a wall in front of the entrance, breeze blocks and plastering on plastering, closed box inside closed box, white 150 x 246 cm, W 24 cm / 57. wall in front of a wall in front of wall in front of a wall, breeze blocks and plastering on plastering, white 536 x 447 cm, W 24 cm, ca. 40 cm distance to the wall in front of a wall / 58. room inside a room within a room inside a room, breeze blocks and plasterboards, wood, plastering on plastering, 3 windows in front of 3 windows, 20 lamps, brown wooden floor above brown wooden floor, white walls in front of white walls and ceiling below ceiling, detached 362 x 888 x 376.5 cm, W 24.40 cm / 59. room inside a room within a room inside a room, plasterboards and chipboards on a wooden construction, plastering on plastering, 3 doors in front of 3 doors, 4 lamps, 1 mirror ball, wooden floor above wooden floor, red carpet on red carpet, white walls in front of white walls and ceiling below ceiling, detached 100 x 320 x 190 cm, W 2.4-20 cm / 60. room inside a room within a room inside a room, plasterboards and chipboards on plasterboards and chipboards on a wooden construction with posts, 2 doors in front of 2 doors, 1 window in front of 1 window, 1 lamp, 1 radiator, floor of lead sheets above floor of lead sheets, grey carpet on grey carpet, white walls in front of white walls and ceilings below ceilings, detached, ca. 30-50 cm distance to the outer room outside the room 268 x 398 x 336 cm, W 3-24 cm / 61. room inside a room within a room inside a room, breeze blocks in a wooden construction, plastering on plastering, 1 door in front of 1 door, concrete floor above concrete floor, white walls in front of white walls and ceiling below ceiling, detached 64 x 90.5 x 174 cm, W 24 cm / 62. wall in front of a wall behind a wall in front of a wall, plasterboards on plasterboards on a wooden construction, 1 window in front of 1 window, white 240 x 351 cm, W 25-70 cm / 63. wall in front of a wall behind a wall in front of a wall, plasterboards on plasterboards on a wooden construction, white 60 x 351 cm, W 25 cm / 64. ceiling above a ceiling above a ceiling above a ceiling, fibreboard in front of fibreboard on wood on top of wood, white 340 x 450 cm, W 5

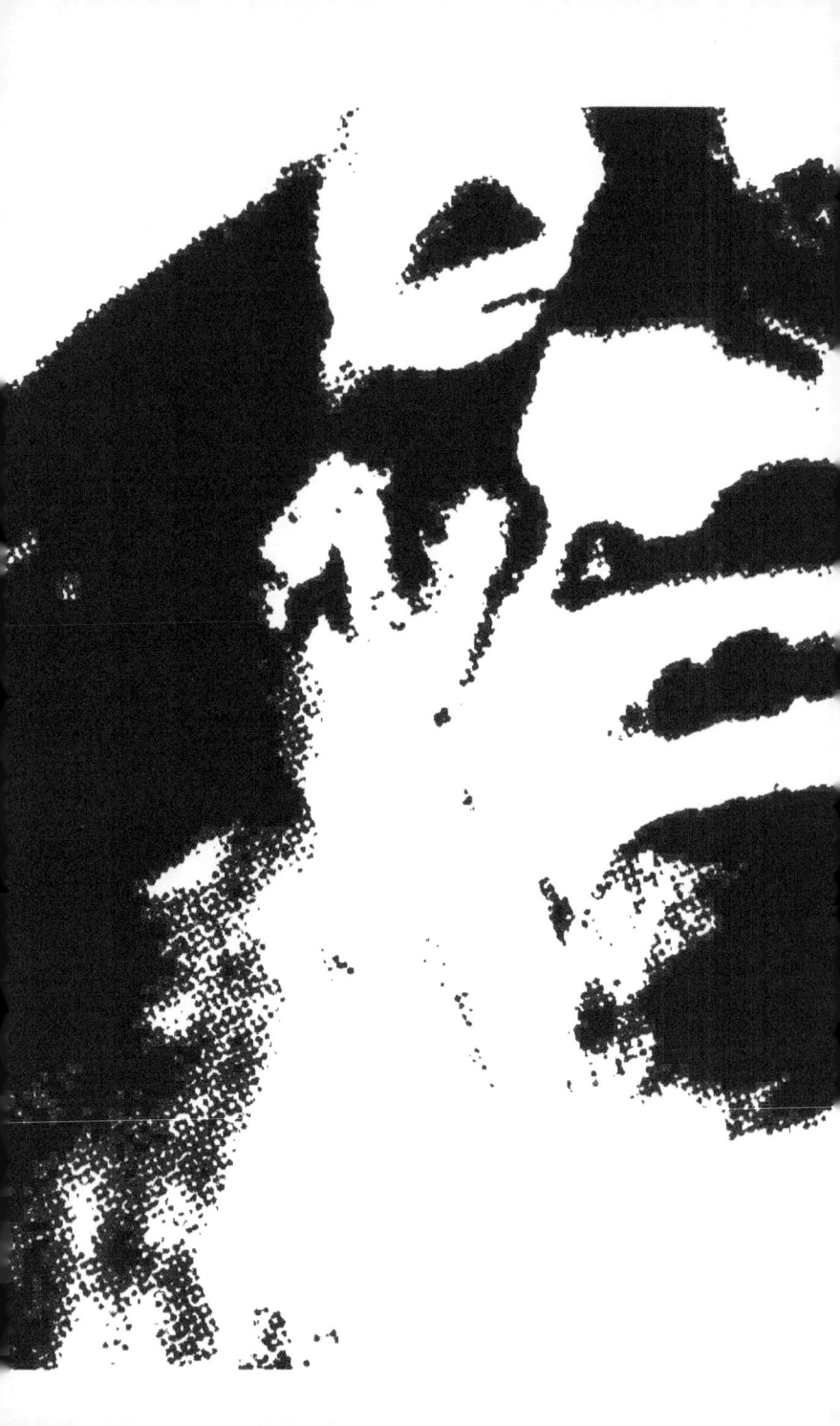

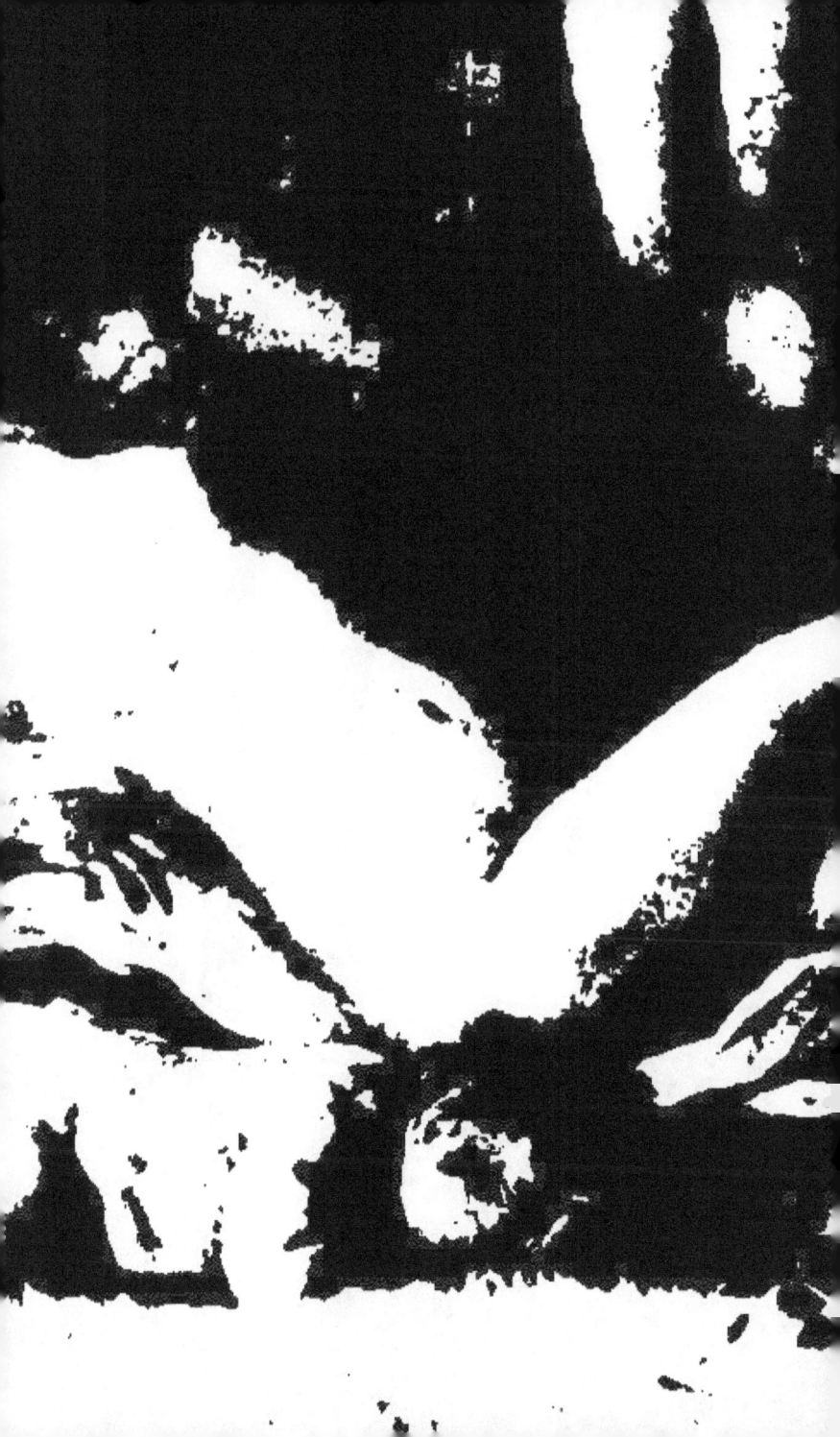

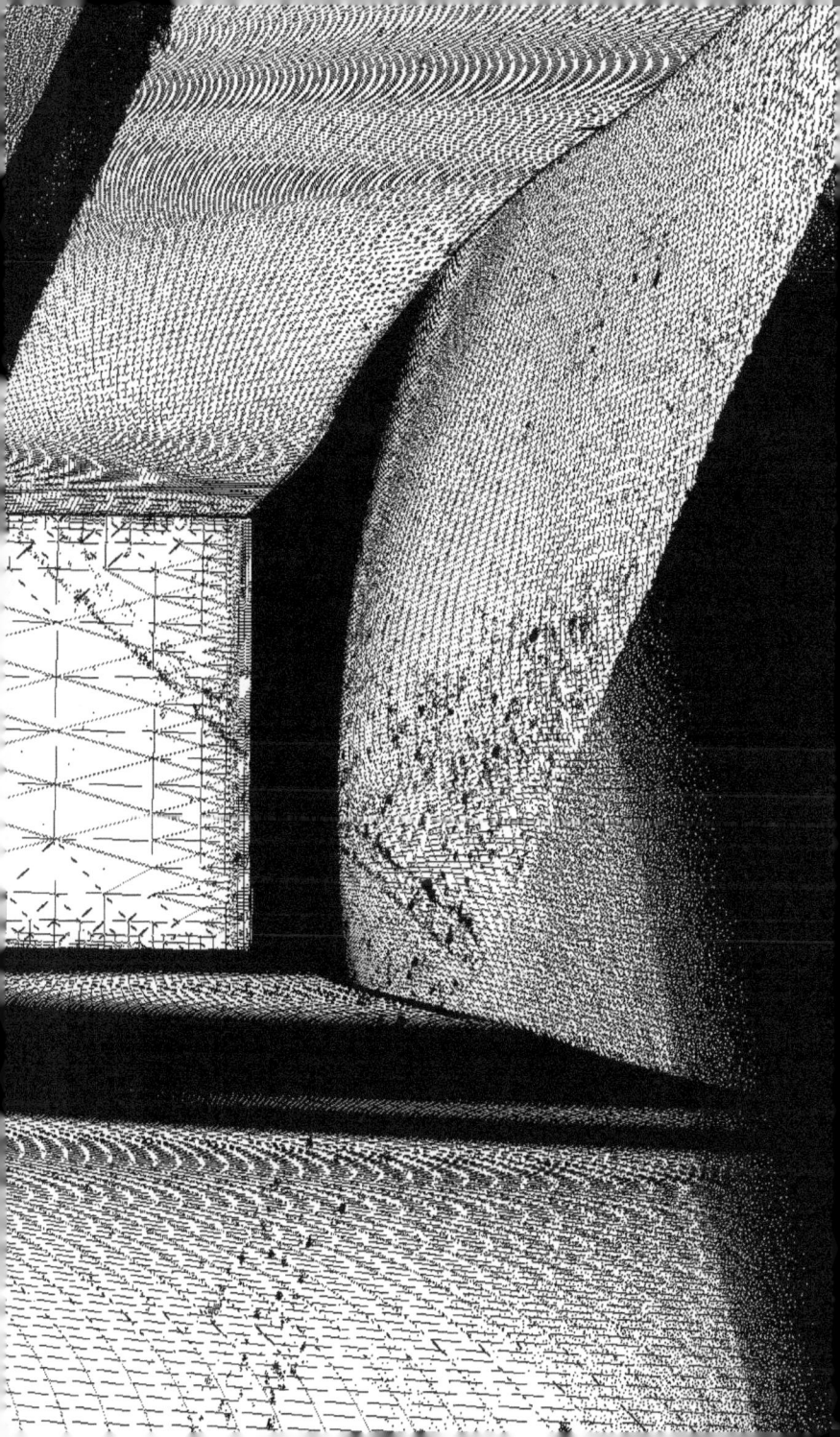

I enter the house inside the house inside the house alone.

I make my way through a kitchen and a living room inside another kitchen inside another kitchen and another living room inside another living room, up to the claustrophobic bathroom and bedroom inside another bathroom inside a bathroom and another bedroom inside a bedroom with no windows on the first floor, and down to the dark spaces in front of more dark spaces in front of more dark spaces of the basement inside a basement inside a basement.

There is the same downbeat furniture and décor in front of décor in front of décor, the same marks in front of marks in front of marks on the carpets and walls on top of carpets and walls on top of carpets and walls, the identical bland magnolia over bland magnolia over bland magnolia and wood-panelled hallways inside wood-panelled hallways inside wood-panelled hallways.

I open a fridge inside a fridge inside a fridge (processed cheese triangles inside other cheese triangles inside other cheese triangles, bottled gherkins inside bottled gherkins inside bottled gherkins), rattle through three layers of bead curtain into another living room inside a living room inside a living room inside a living room inside a living room and sit on a brown sofa containing another brown sofa containing another brown sofa. The last two rooms inside rooms inside rooms are the same, down to the smallest details: the same number of cigarette ends inside cigarette ends inside cigarette ends in the ashtrays one on top of the other on top of the other. There is the same jar of Vaseline inside another jar of Vaseline inside another jar of Vaseline and the same slimming pills inside different sleeping pills inside different sleeping pills in the bathroom cabinet in front of the bathroom cabinet in front of the bathroom cabinet. The same spot wiped clean on the wall at the turn of the stairs lays over another exactly similar spot over another exactly similar spot wiped clean on a wall behind a wall behind a wall at the turn of the stairs behind the turn of the stairs behind the turn of the stairs, the same cloying, unhealthy smells and viscous puddles hide in other smells and puddles hiding in other smells and puddles in a basement inside a basement inside a basement. But they are not exactly identical.

Still no framed photographs of loved ones, keepsakes, kids' pictures over pictures over pictures and scribbles over scribbles over scribbles. But there are children here, somewhere or other. I hear a baby crying from inside another baby from inside another baby, inconsolable and far away, when I go down to a basement beneath a basement beneath a basement—unless it is just the wind howling in the flue inside the flue inside the flue. There is another room inside a room inside a room down there, with unopened packs of kitchen towels, biscuits, lollipops, stacked like gifts or as if for a game in front of more unopened packs of kitchen towels, biscuits, lollipops. I see a safety gate in front of a safety gate in front of a safety gate at the top of the stairs above the stairs above the stairs, the baby's changing mat in a bedroom inside a bedroom inside a bedroom. And the layers of sexual graffiti, spied through a keyhole in front of a keyhole in front of a keyhole, in an attic inside an attic inside an attic. There is a child inside a child inside a child wrapped in a black plastic bag inside a black plastic bag inside a black plastic bag in a bedroom inside a bedroom inside a bedroom.

There is a landscape painted over a landscape painted over a landscape turned to a wall in front of a wall in front of a wall against a living room wainscot on wainscot on wainscot. And nail holes inside nail holes inside nail holes, and nails on top of nails on top of nails without pictures inside of pictures inside of pictures in a hall corridor wall in front of a hall corridor wall in front of a hall corridor wall. It is as though pictures inside of pictures are prohibited here. But the house inside the house inside the house—renovated, refurbished, restored and distressed to an exact pitch of wear and use and unwholesomeness as that renovated, refurbished, restored and distressed to an exact pitch of wear and use and unwholesomeness lying beneath it and beneath that—is full of forbidden images of forbidden images of forbidden images. In fact, the entire house inside the house inside the house is an image inside an image inside an image, a duplicated duplication of a duplication, living image of an image of an image of itself in front of itself and its occupants inside occupants inside occupants, whose stairs within stairs within stairs I tramp, whose threshold over a threshold over a threshold I cross or recoil from, whose basements inside basements inside basements I crawl about in.

The more I know about what I know, the worse the worseness gets.

It is difficult not to project a narrative inside a narrative inside a narrative as I go up and down the stairs over stairs over stairs, step into a malodorous and malevolent bedroom inside a malodorous and malevolent bedroom inside a malodorous and malevolent bedroom, its cloying bower of nasty textures over nasty textures over nasty textures, grim wallpaper over grim wallpaper over grim wallpaper, gilded fittings around gilded fittings around gilded fittings and a mirrored fitted wardrobe in front of a mirrored fitted wardrobe in front of a mirrored fitted wardrobe. Who is the child inside the child inside the child in a corner inside a corner inside a corner, sitting between a bed and a wall in front of a wall in front of a wall, a bin bag over a bin bag over a bin bag that rustles as it breathes? I nudge a foot outside a foot outside a foot to see if it is real.

Water's running in a bathroom inside a bathroom inside a bathroom. The house inside the house inside the house is brought to life in the squeak of a dishcloth around a dishcloth around a dishcloth on a wet plate on a wet plate on a wet plate, a cough after a cough after a cough in a distant room inside a room inside a room, the tink of cutlery, the pained groans as of a man inside a man inside a man masturbating. As if the setting inside the setting inside the setting itself weren't enough—the dour brown-and-cream paintwork over dour brown-and-cream paintwork over dour brown-and-cream paintwork, a soulless emptiness inside a soulless emptiness inside a soulless emptiness, a meagre pleasureless pleasurelessness at the pleasurelessness of it all.

There's nothing here to alleviate the stultifying air of boredom and implied violence, save copies of copies of the Sun and telly guide. In a basement inside a basement inside a basement a cot mattress inside a cot mattress inside a cot mattress is carefully laid in a coal hole inside a coal hole inside a coal hole.

The house inside the house inside the house is a labyrinth inside a labyrinth inside a labyrinth of insulated, soundproofed rooms inside rooms inside rooms—rooms inside rooms inside rooms for every imaginable and unimaginable purpose inside rooms inside rooms inside rooms for every imaginable purpose. Rooms inside rooms inside rooms for a living death, with walls in front of walls in front of walls built in front of walls in front of walls in front of walls in front of walls, pointless corridors inside corridors inside corridors, blind windows in front of blind windows in front of blind windows, rotating rooms inside rotating rooms inside rotating rooms and rooms inside rooms inside rooms from which, if you are accidentally locked in, there is no escape.

The leaden atmosphere is too familiar to me: a timbre of a timbre of a timbre of extreme sadness about sadness about sadness, repressed feelings about repressed feelings about repressed feelings, secrets about secrets about secrets, the unspoken unspokeness.

I can't avoid the avoidance of avoiding myself in here. My living of my living of my life, like some dreadful trauma about trauma about trauma, is endlessly replayed without resolution or consolation.

I enter rooms inside rooms inside rooms only to experience another uncanny twin of a twin of a twin. It is sinister in its little details inside details inside details: like dirty mattresses around dirty mattresses around dirty mattresses, and little cracks in the walls in front of cracks in the walls in front of cracks in the walls.

As a latch over a latch over a latch on the door in front of a door in front of a door to a small room inside a room inside a room quietly clicks shut, leaving me alone in the gloomy light behind the light behind the light, a queasy sense of trepidation sets in. Walking down a carpeted hallway inside a carpeted hallway inside a carpeted hallway, I can hear the sound of dishes being rewashed in an adjacent room inside a room inside a room. Faced with the choice of entering and proceeding either up the stairs over the stairs over the stairs or, worse, down into an even murkier basement inside a basement inside a basement, I pause by a door in front of a door in front of a door in front of a door in front of a door, take a deep breath and enter and enter again and again.

Behind a door behind a door behind a door is another kitchen inside a kitchen inside a kitchen that leads through beaded curtains behind beaded curtains behind beaded curtains into another dingy, stale living-room inside a living room inside a living room. With no response to my 'hello! hello! hello!' I feel invisible thrice over. I rummage through cupboards in front of cupboards in front of cupboards, drawers inside drawers inside drawers and shelves that are shelved.

Grimy flock wallpaper over grimy flock wallpaper over grimy flock wallpaper chokes the rooms inside rooms inside rooms. Shabby thick brown carpet over shabby thick brown carpet over shabby thick brown carpet smothers floors on top of floors on top of floors. Every detail, down to the last cheap brass drawer handle, is pure British kitchen-sink-inside-kitchen-sink-inside-kitchen-sink misery. Upstairs, is another clammy, humid bathroom inside another clammy, humid bathroom inside another clammy, humid bathroom. In a bedroom inside a bedroom inside a bedroom another small figure around a figure around a figure sits calmly inside a bin liner inside a bin liner inside a bin liner. A small mattress on a mattress in another putrid-smelling basement inside a basement inside a basement suggests some third layer of unspeakable abuse.

In the grim, tobacco-stained tobacco stain oppressiveness of a room inside a room inside a room are plastic carrier bags full of plastic carrier bags full of plastic carrier bags full of identical items, books around books around books stacked in exactly the same way. There are giant cages inside cages: 2 x 2 metre cells inside cells inside cells containing an air mattress in an air mattress in an air mattress, a beach umbrella inside a beach umbrella inside a beach umbrella and a black plastic garbage bag inside a black plastic garbage bag inside a black plastic garbage bag. I move deeper inside the building inside the building inside the building, reshaping it piece by piece with constant additions to additions to additions until it becomes a complex organic structure within a structure within a structure, no longer conceivable as a whole inside a whole inside a whole. The indeterminate purpose of a purpose of a purpose and function of a function of a function of the cells inside cells inside cells positions them between what is between comfort and isolation, safety and imprisonment. The structure within the structure within the structure becomes apparent once I am deeper inside the insides. The transparent walls in front of transparent walls in front of transparent walls give a false impression of expanded vision and orientation. Some doors in front of doors in front of doors are locked; others lead into open cells within cells within cells, creating confusing paths inside paths inside paths and passageways inside passageways inside passageways.

A photo in front of a photo in front of a photo on a wall in front of a wall in front of a wall shows what seems to be a reflection of a reflection of a reflection in a mirror inside a mirror inside a mirror, perhaps showing a bin bag inside a bin bag inside a bin bag in a dark corner in a dark corner in a dark corner. As I leave this room inside a room inside a room I'm nervous, I feel people are staring at me. A photo in front of a photo in front of a photo shows a black-clad woman with long dark hair wearing yellow rubber gloves in a kitchen inside a kitchen inside a kitchen in front of a black-clad woman with long dark hair wearing yellow rubber gloves in front of a black-clad woman with long dark hair wearing yellow rubber gloves. I am glimpsing her through a door behind a door behind a door held slightly ajar.

The narrow corridors inside corridors inside corridors are even more claustrophobic. I hesitate in the doorways inside doorways inside doorways but the house inside the house inside the house forces me on.

There's the same sexual graffiti over sexual graffiti over sexual graffiti in the next attic above the attic above the attic, visible only through a keyhole of a locked door behind a keyhole of a locked door behind a keyhole of a locked door, with a locked child-gate placed in front of it and another locked child-gate and another. The control and direction of every minute detail of every detail of every detail is complete and unyielding.

The outside of the house outside the house outside the house had presented a normal face in front of a face in front of a face to the world outside the world outside the world. Inside there's this inescapable feeling of feeling of feeling that I've just missed the replay of a replay some horrific event, or that violence has again been perpetrated here. I hear footsteps over the top of footsteps over the top of footsteps from my vantage point near the attic above the attic above the attic.

I go downstairs and into a tiny room inside a tiny room inside a tiny room, claustrophobic with its low ceiling underneath its ceiling underneath its ceiling. The carpeting on carpeting on carpeting muffles all sound. A third pile of sweets and biscuits suggest the possible presence of a third child. A picture inside a picture inside a picture is turned to a wall in front of a wall in front of a wall, in a hallway inside a hallway inside a hallway outside nails on nails on nails jut from a wall in front a wall in front of a wall as if others have been removed.

There is something that exists on a level behind a layer behind a layer that's hard to isolate but quite easy to feel, crawling just beneath my skin beneath my skin beneath my skin. And whatever it is, replicates entire rooms inside rooms inside rooms (down to the hairline fractures on hairline fractures on hairline fractures in the ceiling plaster over the ceiling plaster over the ceiling plaster) and sits motionless inside a plastic garbage bag inside a black plastic garbage bag inside a black plastic garbage bag in a stifling bedroom inside a bedroom inside a bedroom for hours at a time.

I recall photographing the site behind the site behind the site of a murder to detect some residue of the residue of the residue of the violent act. I imagine digging up the remains of ten girls and young women on top of ten other girls and young women on top of ten other girls and young women who had been tortured to death. I find several shallow graves inside shallow graves inside shallow graves under the floor above the floor above the floor of a child's basement playroom inside a basement inside a basement playroom (which someone has recently renovated). Whatever residue there is here is too persistent simply to cover up with a new basement floor and a fresh patio over an older basement floor and an older patio over an older basement floor and an older patio.

Someone has been adding walls in front of walls in front of walls, doubling rooms inside rooms inside rooms, limiting light sources, channeling air currents and odors, and conjuring new spaces inside of spaces inside of spaces seemingly from nowhere. I have the feeling that I am just another material inside another material inside another material in this grandly unnerving composition inside a composition inside a composition.

Not only are the dark paintwork and net curtains in front of more dark paintwork and more net curtains in front of more dark paintwork and more net curtains in here the same (that, after all, could be coincidence) as in the previous room inside a room inside a room, but the same piles on top of piles on top of piles of black rubbish bags inside black rubbish bags inside black rubbish bags, arranged in the same way, are stacked for removal.

A feeling of indescribable apprehension descends over me, a not so irrational sense that the house is swallowing me up.

I can't identify the smell that permeates these gloomy, comfortless rooms inside rooms inside rooms, but it is sweet, getting sweeter, and curiously unclean.

I imagine myself to be a ghost inside a ghost inside a ghost revisiting the scene of its own murder, moving silently from room inside room inside room to room inside room inside room, experiencing a sickening sense of refracted déjà vu.

At first I can't wholly account for the clammy fear I feel in the latest master bedroom inside the earlier master bedroom inside the earlier master bedroom. Then I realize it has no windows. A nursery inside a nursery inside a nursery is locked and a windowless basement room inside a windowless basement room inside a windowless basement room is stocked with lollipops and pastries, but still no children. And when I ask the question, I notice a dark stain around a dark stain around a dark stain leaking from a black bin bag inside a black bin bag inside a black bin bag. Is it my imagination, or do the floors of the cellars feel strangely sticky?

I let a door behind a door behind a door close behind me. I see what lies behind a heavy bookcase behind a heavy bookcase behind a heavy bookcase pulled away from the far wall in front of the far wall in front of the far wall.

The entrance hall inside the entrance hall inside the entrance hall outside is filled with a video projection over a video projection over a video projection of a steel door in front of a steel door in front of a steel door leading to an aseptic corridor inside an aseptic corridor inside an aseptic corridor with a series of fake doors in front of fake doors in front of fake doors, reproducing a hallway inside a hallway inside a hallway of a high-security prison inside a high-security prison inside a high-security prison. It smells of disinfectant; it's oppressively silent.

The next room inside a room inside a room is a chamber inside a chamber inside a chamber made out of corrugated iron in front of corrugated iron in front of corrugated iron with a floor drain inside a floor drain inside a floor drain. Then comes a refrigerated room inside a refrigerated room inside a refrigerated room. What kind of torture took place behind these closed doors in front of doors in front of doors? How much blood was poured down that drain inside a drain inside a drain? Is the cold room inside a cold room inside a cold room a space to keep bodies inside bodies inside bodies or does it provide another torture method?

In another windowless linoleum-covered room inside another windowless linoleum-covered room inside another windowless linoleum-covered room, a children's pink mattress inside a mattress inside a mattress is the only piece of furniture. It automatically triggers more and more and more disturbing associations.

I am walking in the dark, until I reach a shabby living room inside a living room inside a living room and a bedroom inside a bedroom inside a bedroom with cheap ingrain wallpaper on top of cheap ingrain wallpaper on top of cheap ingrain wallpaper, and a grey-plastered garage inside a grey-plastered garage inside a grey-plastered garage in a moldy smelling basement inside a basement inside a basement with an oil tank inside an oil tank inside an oil tank.

I postulate that someone has removed the rooms inside of rooms inside of rooms from other houses inside of houses inside of houses and built them into this space. Or has reproduced copies of copies of copies of existing rooms inside rooms inside rooms here. The rooms inside rooms inside rooms are always closed, often soundproofed, and they almost never open onto the outside outside the outside outside the outside. One exception is a mud room inside a mud room inside a mud room, which includes a clay basin around a clay basin around a clay basin and a hole around a hole around a hole in the ceiling below the ceiling below the ceiling. It can rain and snow in it; it was conceived to rot.

I am standing in a corridor inside a corridor inside a corridor waiting to go through a set of white double doors in front of white double doors in front of white double doors. All I know about what happens beyond these doors in front of doors in front of doors is that I'll be alone.

I find myself in a brightly lit corridor inside a brightly lit corridor inside a brightly lit corridor that has been painted white over white over white. Even the floor is white over white over white. Walking carefully towards a set of double doors in front of double doors in front of double doors at the end in front of the end in front of the end, I pull them open—to reveal another empty, white corridor inside another white corridor inside another white corridor.

A door behind a door behind a door on my left leads to an empty room inside an empty room inside an empty room, white on white on white again, but this time painted with gloss paint. It makes the sound of my footsteps echo three times. Retreating back out to the corridor inside the corridor inside the corridor, I step through a third set of white doors in front of more white doors in front of more white doors.

This time, I find myself in a small, black room inside a small, black room inside a small black room. In the dim light, I realize there are human shapes inside human shapes inside human shapes inside. Some are standing. Some are crouching. Some shuffle slightly. Not one of them looks at me.

The walls are metal on top of metal on top of metal, like those of a shipping container inside a shipping container inside a shipping container, and the air is warm. I step cautiously past the shapes around shapes around shapes. My heart is still pumping with the repeated shock of entering a room inside a room inside a room. I find myself laughing again.

The house inside the house inside the house has more false corridors inside false corridors inside false corridors, secret rooms inside secret rooms inside secret rooms, and rooms inside rooms inside rooms where once the door behind the door behind the door closes, it will never open again unless I return from the other side.

I'm in a simple room inside a room inside a room flooded with light, with a wooden floor over a wooden floor over a wooden floor. It is a copy of a copy of a copy of a room inside a room inside a room I've seen before. Any minute it could be dismantled and reinstalled somewhere else in the house inside the house inside the house. This is the wrong place for someone nearing the end of their days who wants to die after they die in a humane and harmonious environment.

I will die in one of these rooms inside rooms inside rooms.

I question whether the house's suburban exterior around its exterior around its exterior remains unchanged, when its interior inside its interior inside its interior has undergone so many alterations: walls in front of walls in front of walls in front of walls in front of walls in front of walls in front of walls, ceilings in front of ceilings in front of ceilings under ceilings under ceilings in front of ceilings in front of ceilings, rooms inside rooms inside rooms within rooms inside rooms inside rooms; cupboards inside cupboards inside cupboards morphed into doors in front of doors in front of doors and doors in front of doors in front of doors onto dead ends in front of dead ends in front of dead ends; leaded floors over leaded floors over leaded floors and soundproof chambers inside soundproof chambers inside soundproof chambers.

I continue through a deliberate series of bleak, small rooms inside bleak, small rooms inside bleak, small rooms connected by tight, mangled in-between spaces inside other in-between spaces inside other in-between spaces. I pause in the rooms inside rooms inside rooms that have the familiar makings of a bedroom inside a bedroom inside a bedroom, a dining room inside a dining room inside a dining room. The in-between connective corridors inside corridors inside corridors are confusing, a jumbled network inside a network inside a network that turns the domestic interior inside the interior inside the interior into a treacherous maze inside a maze inside a maze of trickery.

I still remember seeing skulls inside skulls inside skulls inside a room inside a room inside a room inside a room, despite the fact that there were none there.

The house is reproducing existing rooms inside rooms inside rooms in the same places inside the same places.

Through another door behind another door behind another door I arrive in the same house inside the house inside the house with its stairs over stairs over stairs, doors in front of doors in front of doors, rooms inside rooms inside rooms; standard issue, stultifyingly familiar. The change of location is abrupt and total, from the corridors inside corridors inside corridors into unremittingly ordinary rooms inside ordinary rooms inside ordinary rooms. As though I had seen it all before. Behind one door behind another door behind another door a small room inside a small room inside a small room with a mattress inside a mattress inside a mattress and roller blinds in front of roller blinds in front of roller blinds down, some artificial light penetrating through the slits in front of slits in front of slits: a bedroom inside a bedroom inside a bedroom; a tiny grubby room inside a tiny grubby room inside a tiny grubby room, a closet behind a closet behind a closet behind a stained blanket behind a stained blanket behind a stained blanket; elsewhere the last hole inside a hole inside a hole; a destroyed room inside a destroyed room inside a destroyed room, lined with lead sheeting on top of lead sheeting on top of lead sheeting and fibreglass insulation over fibreglass insulation over fibreglass insulation, studs on studs on studs on the floor over the floor over the floor and on the walls in front of walls in front of walls in preparation for more cladding over more cladding over more cladding: the shell around the shell around the shell that is left after the removal of the totally insulated guest room inside the guest room inside the guest room; cellar rooms inside cellar rooms inside cellar rooms, a cellar window in front of a cellar window in front of a cellar window; some kind of a party cellar inside a party cellar inside a party cellar with bare white walls in front of bare white walls in front of bare white walls, colored lights and a disco ball: a whorehouse inside a whorehouse inside a whorehouse; rooms inside rooms inside rooms reserved for something only hinted at; a step down from a jacked-up floor over a jacked-up floor over a jacked-up floor—under it ragged clothing, rubbish, the skin of a collapsible boat inside the skin of a collapsible boat inside the skin of a collapsible boat, a floppy sex doll around a floppy sex doll around a floppy sex doll, deflated—into a messy kitchen inside a messy kitchen inside a messy kitchen with a stainless steel sink on top of a stainless steel sink on top of a stainless steel sink and some crockery; hidden deeper inside the house inside the house inside the house inside the house—I have to bend down, crawl, to get through to it—a bright, clinically lit room inside a room inside a room containing a bed with white sheets on white sheets on white sheets, a bath tub in a bath tub in a bath tub, a cupboard with glasses in front of a cupboard with glasses in front of a cupboard with glasses, remains of food around remains of food around remains of food and a built-in washbasin in a washbasin in a washbasin: a love nest inside a love nest inside a love nest; an old-fashioned wooden staircase on top of a wooden staircase on top of a wooden staircase from the ground floor on top of the ground floor on top of the ground floor to the first floor on top of the first floor on top of the first floor; a small hallway inside a hallway inside a hallway with nine doors, to the stairwell inside the stairwell inside the stairwell, up five or six steps on top of steps on top of steps to a slightly higher coffee room inside a coffee room inside a coffee room with illuminated windows in front of illuminated windows in front of illuminated windows and curtains in front of curtains in front of curtains moving gently in the air, to a somewhat larger room inside a somewhat larger room inside a somewhat larger room which is used as a studio. It is disconcerting to find these overly familiar-seeming rooms inside rooms inside rooms built into this pavilion inside a pavilion inside a pavilion, to go through certain rooms inside rooms inside rooms only to come unexpectedly upon more rooms inside rooms inside rooms tucked into the body of the house inside the house inside the house, amorphous and organic in its depths and defying comprehension. These are rooms inside rooms inside rooms that previously existed elsewhere in the house inside the house inside the house, that were moved or rebuilt there.

The sequence inside the sequence inside the sequence of the rooms inside rooms inside rooms is no longer the same. The top floor above the top floor above the top floor of the house outside the house outside the house is missing, parts of rooms inside the rooms inside the rooms have been constructed that never existed. But it is still the house inside the house inside the house. Certain items, the socks in the corner inside the corner inside the corner, lie in exactly the same place in one room inside a room inside a room as they do in other rooms inside rooms inside rooms. The house inside the house inside the house is never guaranteed as authentic by a final state.

The house inside the house inside the house is a bewildering sequence inside a sequence inside a sequence of rooms inside rooms inside rooms designed for all the activities of ordinary living and filled with the signs of a bachelor existence, from the inflatable dolls inside dolls inside dolls to the electric cooking rings around electric cooking rings around electric cooking rings, from a studio inside a studio inside a studio to a ripped out guest room inside a ripped out guest room inside a ripped out guest room, from the rubbish lying around to the built-in washbasin in the built-in washbasin in the built-in washbasin —as though anyone who had once used these things that wasn't me had not been there for a long time.

A torn up floor above a floor above a floor, a completely insulated room inside a completely insulated room inside a completely insulated room, a room inside a room inside a room in a room inside a room inside a room, a ceiling under a ceiling under a ceiling under a ceiling under a ceiling under a ceiling under a ceiling, a wall in front of a wall in front of a wall in front of a wall in front of a wall in front of a wall in front of a wall, 4 walls in front of 4 walls in front of 4 walls in front of a wall in front of a wall in front of a wall in front of a wall, 6 wall pieces in front of 6 wall pieces in front of 6 wall pieces in front of another wall in front of another wall in front of another wall, a pillar around a pillar around a pillar, a section of wall in front of a section of wall in front of a section of wall underneath the fourth ceiling underneath the ceiling underneath the ceiling, a removed and replaced section of wall in front of a removed and replaced section of wall in front of a removed and replaced section of wall between the walls in front of walls in front of walls.

I imagine living entombed in the house inside the house inside the house for years in almost total isolation.

I imagine someone has come in because a door behind a door behind a door is left open. They drink a cup of coffee after a cup of coffee after a cup of coffee with me. We have a boring conversation about a boring conversation, they leave again and again, and don't even wonder why they were here in the first place.

I might open a wrong door behind a door behind a door at the wrong moment and plunge into an abyss inside an abyss inside an abyss. Whether I leave this room inside a room inside a room or stay, it is perfectly possible that I am not conscious of what is happening to me.

The non-recognizability is part of its construction strategy, which involves 'doubling' and multiplying rooms or parts of rooms inside themselves: wall in front of wall in front of wall in front of wall in front of wall in front of wall, ceiling below ceiling below ceiling below ceiling below ceiling below ceiling, floor on floor on floor on floor on floor on floor, room in room in room in room in room in room. It is a labor of representation of representation of representation of representation that uses the same or similar materials to replicate in the same place inside the same place inside the same place something that already exists there, beneath one or more layers inside layers inside layers. The representation of representation of representation is located exactly in front of the thing in front of the thing in front of the thing it is representing.

The room inside the room inside the room I'm in has one solid red plaster block around a red plaster block around a red plaster block and one solid black one around another solid black one around another solid black one in a wall in front of a wall in front of a wall in front of an existing wall in front of a wall in front of a wall; the coffee room inside the coffee room inside the coffee room, in which I spend an uneventful half-hour. It might in the meantime have completed three 360° rotations. A guest room inside a guest room inside a guest room has a three-metre-thick layer of insulation inside a two-metre thick layer of insulation inside a two-metre thick layer of insulation. Differences, sources of possibly unexpected effects are relegated behind the walls behind the walls behind the walls of the visible rooms inside rooms inside rooms, and thereby put beyond the reach of normal perception.

Existing rooms inside rooms inside rooms continue to be hidden by the same strategy of production that conceals itself in the act of the replication of replication of replication.

I enter in between newly constructed sections in front of newly constructed sections in front of newly constructed sections and the original walls in front of walls in front of walls, doubled windows in front of double windows in front of double windows in front of a solid wall in front of a solid wall in front of a solid wall, moving wall sections in front of moving wall sections in front of moving wall sections and narrow passageways inside narrow passageways inside narrow passageways, contorted routes within routes within routes between rooms inside of rooms inside of rooms. There is no way to distinguish between the original of the original of the original and the double of the double of the double, between the first structure of the structure of the structure and the new construction of the new construction of the new construction, between the existing architecture inside the existing architecture inside the existing architecture and the added-on work in front of the added-on work in front of the added-on work. I can't distinguish any more between what has been added to the additions to the additions and what has been subtracted from the subtractions from the subtractions. The only way now is to again measure the hidden spaces inside the hidden spaces inside the hidden spaces. I can't get to the original structure outside the structure outside the structure any more without systematically drilling apart and destroying the house inside the house inside the house.

Its source is not in the rooms inside the rooms inside the rooms themselves, however disquieting these may be. It lies behind what is behind them, in the area behind the area behind the area without access, or, if it were possible to reenter it, where it is impossible to tell what I am up against. The inward doubling of rooms inside rooms inside rooms in this house inside this house inside this house, just like the construction of rooms inside rooms inside rooms which could have been there before but were possibly not really there—this replication of the replication of the replication of what is actually or virtually there—also generates places outside of places outside of places inhabited by this unseen something inside an unseen something inside an unseen something. The sinking of architectural elements inside architectural elements inside architectural elements and whole rooms inside rooms inside rooms into a second, deeper layer of space in front of a third deeper layer of space in front of a fourth deep layer of space tips the over-familiar, the things inside things inside things that are no longer perceived in their own right and which can thus stand for a home inside a home inside a home, into a negation of themselves. Anything of my own is again rendered inaccessible and unidentifiable.

It is located on the other side of familiar places inside familiar places inside familiar places: as the unfathomable basis of the latter it is the place inside the place inside the place where I cannot be. But it places figures inside figures inside figures in the space inside of space inside of space behind in-built rooms behind in-built rooms behind in-built rooms. Figures inside of figures inside of figures are placed in inaccessible areas inside inaccessible areas inside inaccessible areas, or rather, left there, like the coffin inside the coffin inside the coffin, the puddle around the puddle around the puddle, the piss corner in the piss corner in the piss corner, the white sphere inside the white sphere inside the white sphere, the black star inside the black star inside the black star (negative cores), the pillar inside the pillar inside the pillar, the slime tub in the slime tub in the slime tub, stones in stones in stones.

Whether to remain transfixed by the normality of the coffee room inside the coffee room inside the coffee room, a delusion of a delusion of a delusion of domesticity, or to sink further into the house inside the house inside the house. I am the between moving between these six places within places within places.

An important wall in front of a wall in front of a wall with behind-the-wall pictures in front of behind-the-wall pictures in front of behind-the-wall pictures of the space behind the space behind the space between the walls in front of the walls in front of the walls. Sometimes I get behind them myself. I make a place inside a place inside a place of my own between the in-built structures inside the in-built structures inside the in-built structures and the other, cut-off places behind the cut-off places behind the cut-off places, I move to and fro between them. I continue to document this six-fold access in photos of photos of photos and videos of videos of videos.

In the coffee room inside the coffee room inside the coffee room with nothing happening, static; only the curtain in front of the curtain in front of the curtain in front of the illuminated window in front of the illuminated window in front of the illuminated window moving gently in the air from the ventilator in front of the ventilator in front of the ventilator positioned behind the inside wall in front of the wall in front of the wall. The room inside the room inside the room is something other than a normal room inside a normal room inside a normal room, like countless others in apartments inside apartments inside apartments anywhere and everywhere.

I make videos of videos of videos of dark passages inside dark passages inside dark passages, taken with my wildly unsteady hand-held camera and only lit with a flash-lit flashlight. In these it is possible to make out diverse, more or less legible details in front of details in front of details, some frightening items: coloured roots inside roots inside roots proliferating inwards, a human figure in front of a human figure in front of a human figure, a jumbled heap of material outside a jumbled heap of material outside a jumbled heap of material. I hear the sound of someone behind someone behind someone gasping and realize that it is somehow forcing its way through the internal passages inside the internal passages inside the internal passages in this house inside this house inside this house, places inside places inside places that I have never entered.

An interstice inside an interstice inside an interstice between the abyss inside the abyss inside the abyss and the banality of banality of banality, this structure inside a structure inside a structure leaves no room outside a room outside a room for unsuspecting innocence.

Squeezing through ever tighter spaces within spaces within spaces, feeling trapped, rubbing up against clammy walls inside clammy walls inside clammy walls, I feel as if the house inside the house inside the house is actually several houses inside several houses inside several houses. It is made from parts of parts of parts of other houses inside houses inside houses but is also an autonomous thing inside a thing inside a thing. It contains multiple houses inside multiple houses inside multiple houses within itself: wall in front of wall in front of wall in front of wall in front of wall in front of wall, wall in front of wall in front of wall in front of wall in front of wall in front of wall, wall behind wall behind wall behind wall behind wall behind wall, passage inside passage inside passage in room inside room inside room, room inside room inside room in room inside room inside room.

With a change of location inside a location inside a location, the contradiction between the inconsequential ordinariness of a room inside a room inside a room and the abyss inside the abyss inside the abyss on the other side of another side of another side is replaced by an atmosphere of penetrating, alienating alienation. The house inside the house inside the house gains additional levels on top of levels on top of levels of legibility. The house inside the house inside the house is a number of houses inside houses inside houses, each with many rooms inside rooms inside rooms in each room inside a room inside a room, in each room inside a room inside a room innumerable cupboards in front of cupboards in front of cupboards, shelves on top of shelves on top of shelves, boxes in boxes in boxes, and somewhere, in each one of them inside another one inside another one, I am stood.

This is an architecture inside an architecture inside an architecture so turned in on itself that my journey into it leads to dead ends inside dead ends inside dead ends, hazards inside hazards inside hazards: windows in front of windows in front of windows that open only onto other windows in front of windows in front of windows and rooms inside rooms inside rooms bathed in light that appears natural but is actually artificial.

A whole world inside a world inside a world opens up with all sorts of things inside things inside things that are not recognizable but which are there and which influence the way I feel, think, and act, how I live my daily life in here. Cladding on top of cladding on top of cladding in various materials alters the effect of a room inside a room inside a room without me quite being able to say why. Even the smallest protuberances and indentations on top and inside of protuberances and indentations on top and inside of protuberances and indentations on the finished surface in front of the finished surface in front of the finished surface of a wall in front of a wall in front of a wall arouse a response. And when that happens, the effect is registered separately from the cause of the cause of the cause. The affective state is induced, but the means by which it was created remain hidden behind the scenes—in the walls behind the walls behind the walls and under the floors under the floors under the floors under the floors.

Even the smallest grooves inside grooves inside grooves in a layer of plaster in front of a layer of plaster in front of a layer of plaster spur emotions, whereby the impact is perceived as being separate from the cause of the cause of the cause. It can happen, therefore, that I think I'm not feeling well today, although that feeling is being brought on by the room inside the room inside the room, something I cannot know. I observe this, but I never go at it directly.

There are rooms inside of rooms inside of rooms in this house inside this house inside this house that I can no longer access, and therefore can no longer photograph or measure. All that remains are room numbers in front of room numbers in front of room numbers—and a feeling about a feeling about a feeling—but I can't really think about the rooms inside the rooms inside the rooms as if they still existed normally.

I walk into intricate puzzles inside intricate puzzles inside intricate puzzles of family dysfunction, spatial dead ends in front of spatial dead ends in front of spatial dead ends. A room inside a room inside a room calls to mind footage of footage of footage from a police search, and raises the spectre of a world where even the most private areas of my life are increasingly vulnerable to videos of videos of video surveillance. The house inside the house inside the house is an architectural cover-up, an attempt to conceal the past under a veneer of normalized normality.

What is it obscuring behind its facades in front of facades in front of facades? The dwelling inside the dwelling inside the dwelling has been stripped away. The rooms on top of rooms on top of rooms resemble a series of stacked blocks on top of stacked blocks on top of stacked blocks, but close examination reveals architectural details inside architectural details inside architectural details, such as doorknobs inside doorknobs inside doorknobs, light switches in front of light switches in front of light switches, and window frames in front of windows in front of windows incised into the monotone monolith inside the monotone monolith inside the monotone monolith that became a monument to former inhabitants; one could touch the absence of a light switch in front of a light switch in front of a light switch, fingers meeting the ghosts of the future.

Two luminous windows in front of two luminous windows in front of two luminous windows in a room inside a room inside a room bestow a confrontational aliveness. I sometimes feel the windows in front of windows in front of windows in this house inside this house inside this house are looking at me.

I feel that the world behind the world behind the world has suddenly been sucked into a void inside a void inside a void at my back with the closing of a door behind a door behind a door. The sense that spaces inside spaces inside spaces are smaller than they should be, and blocked windows in front of blocked windows in front of blocked windows at several points in the house inside the house inside the house to disconnect a visitor from the exterior of the exterior of the exterior.

There are exposed windows in front of windows in front of windows in the kitchens inside the kitchens inside the kitchens. After leaving I pass through a sitting room inside a sitting room inside a sitting room with lace doilies and shopping items that needed to be put away, and continue upstairs above the upstairs above the upstairs to yet more claustrophobic windowless rooms inside claustrophobic windowless rooms inside claustrophobic windowless rooms.

I excavate further down through the layers of paper on top of paper on top of paper, to uncover a bedroom inside a bedroom inside a bedroom with white walls in front of white walls in front of white walls, a white wardrobe in front of a white wardrobe in front of a white wardrobe, white bedding on white bedding on white bedding, and a thick white carpet on thick white carpet on thick white carpet. Another body inside a body inside a body is propped up in the corner in a black garbage bag inside a black garbage bag inside a black garbage bag. I have been caught in a loop within a loop within a loop.

An attic inside an attic inside an attic, above a bedroom inside a bedroom inside a bedroom, is loaded with symbols of domestic space over symbols of domestic space over symbols of domestic space. But the garret inside the garret inside the garret represents another dead end in front of a dead end in front of a dead end.

A baby gate in front of a baby gate in front of a baby gate in front of the door in front of the door in front of the door provokes more questions. The questions are impossible to answer; the door behind the door behind the door is locked. The attic door behind the attic door behind the attic door is followed by a vertiginous view back down a tight helical staircase inside a tight helical staircase inside a tight helical staircase.

I run down multiple flights of stairs on top of multiple flights of stairs on top of multiple flights of stairs into a basement inside a basement inside a basement, the subterranean area where the most horrific secrets are hidden and hidden again and hidden again. I encounter a small room inside a room inside a room with floral wallpaper on top of floral wallpaper on top of floral wallpaper, and then a doorway behind a doorway behind a doorway to a bleak room inside a bleak room inside a bleak room with twine twisted and hanging on the wall in front of the wall in front of the wall and an overturned chair inside an overturned chair inside an overturned chair. Is it the site of a suicide on top of the site of a suicide on top of the site of a suicide or perhaps a hanging in front of a hanging in front of a hanging? Outside this dark, insulated space outside another dark, insulated space outside another dark, insulated space is a stack of paper towels and cupcakes, like one would find at a child's birthday party. The gaiety, which marks the celebration of a birth, is overshadowed by the distinct feeling the room inside the room inside the room could function as a torture chamber around a torture chamber around a torture chamber.

There is another secret passage inside a secret passage inside a secret passage behind a bookshelf behind a bookshelf behind a bookshelf that has been pulled away from a wall in front of a wall in front of a wall, a low-ceilinged hallway inside a low-ceilinged hallway inside a low-ceilinged hallway brings me to the end of a passageway inside a passageway inside a passageway blocked off by a storeroom door in front of a storeroom door in front of a storeroom door, which is chained and padlocked in place. If the storeroom inside the storeroom inside the storeroom was open, a tiny chamber inside a chamber inside a chamber at the end of the corridor inside the corridor inside the corridor would contain a stained crib mattress on top of a stained crib mattress on top of a stained crib mattress. The sound of a crying baby; innocence suffocated by the depths of this monstrous house inside a house inside a house.

I stare at damage to the walls inside walls inside walls and the floorboards on top of floorboards on top of floorboards. What is that shape inside the shape inside the shape on the wall in front of the wall in front of the wall? A horse head inside a horse head inside a horse head? Australia inside Australia inside Australia? The images become mnemonics for knowledge that ultimately resides outside the house outside the house inside the house inside the house.

Distorted doublings reveal that which has been hidden behind the hidden behind the hidden, and these disturbances to the expected order provoke a re-consideration of the house inside the house inside the house, the home inside the home inside the home, and the domestic realm inside the domestic realm inside the domestic realm.

More creepy basements inside basements inside basements with one bare bulb and unexplainable holes inside of holes inside of holes dug in the middle of the floor on top of the floor on top of the floor; basements inside basements inside basements like this all over, locked up and untouched since the '40s, ignored but not forgotten by the figments of people going about their lives in the rooms inside rooms inside rooms above.

I confront the lies I tell myself to keep living after traumas of unspeakable proportions: the untruths of modern life, spatial and perceptual manipulation through various media—mirrors inside mirrors inside mirrors, photographs inside photographs inside photographs, surveillance video inside surveillance video inside surveillance video.

I don't know where I can go from here. I could go on running on the spot, just go until the house inside the house inside the house pushes me out or swallows me up altogether. I could systematically dismantle the house inside the house inside the house.

It's just chance that out of necessity I'm here. I'd love to get out.

By now the house inside the house inside the house has become independent. It has its own inner dynamics. The sheer amount means that I can't distinguish any more between what has been added to the additions to the additions and what has been subtracted from the subtractions from the subtractions. There is no way now of fully documenting the documenting of the documenting of what has happened in the house inside the house inside the house. The only way now would be to measure the hidden spaces inside the hidden spaces inside the hidden spaces. No-one could get to the original structure outside the structure outside the structure any more without systematically drilling apart and destroying the house inside the house inside the house. The layers of lead inside the layers of lead inside the layers of lead mean you can't even X-ray it.

Because I spend all my time here, I have to accept the rooms inside rooms inside rooms as they are, and accept the most recently built as perfectly normal. And even though the light in this room inside a room inside a room is from a lamp behind a lamp behind a lamp and the air is produced by a ventilator behind a ventilator behind a ventilator, by now the atmosphere seems quite normal to me. I need normal light in front of light in front of light and recirculated air here.

This is the work of something insulating itself.

There are rooms inside rooms inside rooms completely insulated with lead on top of lead on top of lead, glass fibre on glass fibre on glass fibre, sound-proofing materials on sound-proofing materials on sound-proofing materials and other stuff. I am right in the middle of it and surrender to the house inside the house inside the house. Whether I am insulating myself from the world, or whether it's a breakthrough—I don't really know.

All this takes a long time. I wouldn't like it if the only thing about the house inside the house inside the house is that I live in it. Because that would mean it was just my cell inside my cell inside my cell. Whether it's a place of refuge. I don't know. Anyway, now I've got a guest room inside a guest room inside a guest room. Maybe some others might like to fester away here instead of me.

A wall in front of a wall in front of a wall in front of a wall in front of a wall in front of a wall in front of a wall, a wall behind a wall behind a wall behind a wall behind a wall behind a wall behind a wall, a passage inside a passage inside a passage in room inside a room inside a room, a room inside a room inside a room in a room inside a room inside a room, a passage inside a passage inside a passage in a room inside a room inside a room, a wall in front of a wall in front of a wall in front of a wall in front of a wall in front of a wall in front of a wall, a room inside a room inside a room in a room inside a room inside a room, a room inside a room inside a room in a room inside a room inside a room, a room inside a room inside a room in a room inside a room inside a room, a red stone inside a red stone inside a red stone behind a room inside a room inside a room, lead on top of lead on top of lead around a room inside a room inside a room, lead on top of lead on top of lead in a floor beneath a floor beneath a floor, light around a room inside a room inside a room, light around a room inside a room inside a room, a wall in front of a wall in front of a wall in front of a wall in front of a wall in front of a wall in front of a wall, a figure inside a figure inside a figure in a wall in front of a wall in front of a wall, a wall in front of a wall in front of a wall in front of a wall in front of a wall in front of a wall in front of a wall, a wall in front of a wall in front of a wall in front of a wall in front of a wall in front of a wall in front of a wall, a room inside a room inside a room in a room inside a room inside a room, a wall in front of a wall in front of a wall in front of a wall in front of a wall in front of a wall in front of a wall, a wall in front of a wall in front of a wall in front of a wall in front of a wall in front of a wall in front of a wall, a wall in front of a wall in front of a wall in front of a wall in front of a wall in front of a wall in front of a wall, a ceiling under a ceiling under a ceiling under a ceiling under a ceiling under a ceiling, a section of wall in front of a section of wall in front of a section of wall in front of a wall in front of a wall in front of a wall in front of a wall, a wall in front of a wall in front of a wall in front of a wall in front of a wall in front of a wall in front of a wall, a section of wall in front of a section of wall in front of a section of wall in front of a wall in front of a wall in front of a wall in front of a wall, a wall in front of a wall in front of a wall in front of a wall in front of a wall...

I start to build complete rooms inside rooms inside rooms with floors on top of floors on top of floors, walls in front of walls in front of walls and ceilings below ceilings below ceilings, that you can't see as a room inside a room inside a room in a room inside a room inside a room or a room around a room around a room around a room around a room around a room. There is a constant stream of new rooms inside rooms inside rooms made from various materials around various materials around various materials. Some of them—imperceptibly—rise up, sink back down or complete a full rotation. The house inside the house inside the house is really about the fact that I am always starting again.

The first time I built a room inside a room inside a room, I had no idea that's what I had done. It was something else that told me.

I don't notice that the room inside the room inside the room has rotated once right round. Of course I can't know what will happen. I might open the wrong door behind the wrong door behind the wrong door at the wrong moment and plunge into an abyss inside an abyss inside an abyss.

There are rooms inside rooms inside rooms which are not recognisable as such, but which have an effect, change my mood or my way of behaving.

As soon as I have built a stone inside a stone inside a stone into a wall in front of a wall in front of a wall—a red one or a totally black one—after a while I don't know where it is any more, and the same thing happens again and again and again and again. It's like that with a wall in front of a wall in front of a wall and exactly the same with a room inside a room inside a room. As soon as I spend any time in a room inside a room inside a room, I accept it as a normal room inside a room inside a room.

A whole world within a world within a world opens up with all sort of things that are not recognisable but which are there and which influence the way I feel, think and act, how I live my daily life. The fact that the room inside a room inside a room is rotating without my knowing it can alter the direction I walk in. Cladding on top of cladding on top of cladding in various materials around materials around materials can alter the effect of a room inside a room inside a room without me quite being able to say why. Even the smallest protuberances on protuberances on protuberances and indentations in indentations in indentations on the finished surface in front of the surface in front of the surface of a wall in front of a wall in front of a wall can arouse a response in me. And when that happens, the effect is registered separately from the cause of the cause of the cause. So sometimes I might say, I'm having a bad day today: the feeling has been induced by the room inside a room inside a room but I can't know that. I observe these things. But I don't set out to make them happen.

I spend more and more months digging up the whole house inside the house inside the house. I manage to reconstruct one room inside a room inside a room more or less as it was. 8 by 3.76 by 1.25 metres. It has five individual windows in front of windows in front of windows. The ceiling below the ceiling below the ceiling goes up and down continuously, imperceptibly. The room inside the room inside the room remains in place for a whole year. It is brutal work, and when I think about it, it all scarcely seems credible. I try to become even more concentrated, construct poised rooms inside rooms inside rooms, well-balanced. Whatever I take away on one side is put back on the other. Amongst other things I make a pillar inside a pillar inside a pillar, try to get to the point in the house inside the house inside the house. Build a room inside a room inside a room somewhere else almost exactly like the existing room inside a room inside a room here. Go specially all that way and then put it up in eight days.

Do you know the way people on spaceships beam themselves from one place to another? When I am back here again I try to imagine the things that are happening there. I could imagine repeatedly building a more or less identical room inside a room inside a room from memory in various different places inside places inside places, to get back here again maybe. But I don't really know. They look unremarkable and meaningless, but at the same time they freeze everything.

I'm in a big room inside a bigger room inside a bigger room, looking out of a window in front of a window in front of a window. In front of it: a substituted piece of wall in front of a substituted piece of wall in front of a substituted piece of wall.

The motivation is there's nothing else to do. I keep having to test the thing inside the thing inside the thing I have committed myself to, keep having to ask myself the question inside the question inside the question, whether it's at all worth doing.

I tried at one stage not to leave one part of the house inside the house inside the house for an indefinite period. In my search for immediacy I became immediate. When that happens I can't talk. But I also seek out other moments, where I stand next to the self beside myself beside myself.

I am seeking to get closer to things inside things inside things.

There are different layers on top of layers on top of layers that merge into one another—that I can't control.

I was once registered as having a perceptual disorder and as being mentally ill, but I had only told them what I was doing at the time. I didn't lie. I will build more rooms inside more rooms inside more rooms, a room inside a room inside a room that I don't perceive as a room inside a room inside a room in a room inside a room inside a room or a room inside a room inside a room round a room round a room round a room, then suddenly a wall in front of a wall in front of a wall is there and then gone again. I look at a wall in front of a wall in front of a wall and am interested in any unevennesses on its surface in front of its surface in front of its surface: the tiniest hole in the tiniest hole in the tiniest hole, the slightest protuberance on the slightest protuberance on the slightest protuberance.

It even seems illogical to me to build these rooms inside rooms inside rooms at all. I have the feeling that I needn't build them at all.

My experiments involve going into a room inside a room inside a room, leaving it again, hoping that the experience will linger there. Perhaps all these rooms inside rooms inside rooms are also a preparation for my one day not having to enter any more rooms inside rooms inside rooms.

I am interested in distortions. I sit looking at them for hours, for days on end. And then there are screams screamed over screams over screams, they are always there. Repeated screams over screams over screams. I see the human scream screamed over screams over screams. I dig holes inside holes inside holes, bury myself. I hope the screams screamed over screams over screams will stay behind in the room inside the room inside the room after I leave it. Here another female art student has been killed.

I crawl inside totally insulated boxes inside totally insulated boxes inside totally insulated boxes. If I am sitting in a box inside a box inside a box I can't hear the screaming screamed over screams over screams outside any more... I hope that life will be the difference between a full and an empty box inside a box inside a box. I introduce a layer of insulation on top of a layer of insulation on top of a layer of insulation into a room inside a room inside a room. I use my technical skills to completely insulate the room inside the room inside the room as far as the senses are concerned. I come into an unremarkable passage inside a passage inside a passage, then behind a veneered, everyday door in front of a veneered, everyday door in front of a veneered, everyday door, reinforced with steel beams inside steel beams inside steel beams, I am confronted with a cross-section of the insulating materials on top of insulating materials on top of insulating materials. I feel strong pressure on my ears if I bend down into the black, unfathomable depth below the black, unfathomable depth below the black, unfathomable depth. If I had gone into the room inside the room inside the room the door behind the door behind the door would have swung shut. There is no way of opening it either from inside or from outside. I am gone. Whether it is a hole inside a hole inside a hole or a window in front of a window in front of a window, I don't know, I never went in.

A child falls into a deep freeze inside a deep freeze inside a deep freeze, while a woman is standing right next to it doing the washing-up.

I take photos of photos of photos of the place inside the place inside the place where the students were murdered. Later there are flowers laying on flowers laying on flowers there. I keep coming back. And then I come to the conclusion that places inside places inside places just look the same although quite different things have happened there.

One of the doors behind a door behind a door has gone again. One of the doors behind a door behind a door leads to a light, a relatively large room inside a room inside a room that has openings behind openings behind openings to the outside. Up to twelve windows in front of windows in front of windows one in front of the other in order to change the way the light falls. That's why the walls in front of the walls in front of the walls are so thick.

There are several layers of paint on top of paint on top of the paint on the glass in front of the glass in front of the glass. No light gets through. But it creates the impression of a window in front of a window in front of a window. I push this section of wall in front of a section of wall in front of a section of wall in front of it, in front of the opening out to the back.

I am standing in front of an important wall in front of a wall in front of a wall, where I lean the behind-the-wall pictures of the behind-the-wall pictures of the behind-the-wall pictures or the behind-the-wall stones inside the behind-the-wall-stones inside the behind-the-wall-stones or sometimes I get behind it myself. At the moment it is empty.

Of course there are original walls behind the walls behind the walls, otherwise the house outside the house outside the house wouldn't stand up. The colour on top of the colour on top of the colour is not just on the surface of the surface of the surface.

There are leftovers of leftovers of leftovers from buckets of mortar in buckets of mortar in buckets of mortar, or not, some are plaster. Left-over mortar in a bucket inside leftover mortar in a bucket inside leftover mortar in a bucket. I take it in my hand and make it into a ball around a ball around a ball. I end up with twenty or thirty. I stick these all together and that makes one big ball around another big ball around another big ball. It gives me new material to close up a small wall in front of a wall in front of a wall or some opening in an opening in an opening. The other stuff is newspaper, soaked and compressed. Amazingly enough it's super tough, a great material, a great building material, utterly simple material. You can apply thin layers of plaster on top of plaster on top of plaster only consisting of a surface on a surface on a surface. Big boards in front of big boards in front of big boards in front that are made from a lot of smaller parts around a lot of other smaller parts around a lot of other smaller parts, starting again and again and again and again in different places. The amazing thing is that it's simply a matter of doing.

I can stand in front of a wall in front of a wall in front of a wall in front of a wall for hours on end, looking at it. I can do that once, twice, for a whole month or even longer, and then at some point I can tell everyone about that wall.

All this from the sheer boredom of boredom. All jobs involve repeated actions.

The other door behind the door behind the door of the sorting-room inside the sorting-room inside the sorting-room leads into a little room inside a little room inside a little room with a coffee table and also the central switching station inside the central switching station inside the central switching station, the fuse box inside the fuse box inside the fuse box. It's a room inside a room inside a room that can rotate on its own axis. A window in front of a window in front of a window is lit from behind. It has a pleasant, friendly atmosphere, but which is obviously wholly artificial. There is a warm halogen lamp in front of a warm halogen lamp in front of a warm halogen lamp.

I have the feeling again that my brain has stopped and my body is going on turning, tighter and tighter until it tears. The ventilator in front of the ventilator in front of the ventilator is not on at the moment. I like it when there's a gentle flow of air. At the moment I feel more as though the window in front of the window in front of the window is looking at me. Like the two bright windows behind the windows behind the windows outside.

The thing is that I am always waiting to see what will happen. I can never know in advance. Sometimes I have the feeling that people suddenly just appear. And then there might be a kind of vortex inside a vortex inside a vortex, a loud droning noise.

I take yet another door behind a door behind a door off its hinges, the one at the very back. Now I can get behind the rotating room inside the room inside the room. It's very difficult to take photographs of photographs of photographs of the rooms inside the rooms inside the rooms. You partly have to cut the rooms inside the rooms inside the rooms open again.

There are more things stored here. These are quite lightly built walls in front of walls in front of walls that I have already bricked some things into. I always have to be sure that I am not overdoing it.

When I open it I get to a wall in front of a wall in front of a wall that sounds less and less solid.

Some bits are more rickety, some bits are more solid. You can't tell just by tapping. The smaller the room inside the room inside the room, the lighter it is. I can't get any more big, heavy parts into it.

Downstairs a hall inside a hall inside a hall goes to a door behind a door behind a door at the back that leads into a guest room inside a guest room inside a guest room, the heavily insulated room inside the heavily insulated room inside the heavily insulated room. Inside it there is a grille in front of a grille in front of a grille in the wall in front of the wall in front of the wall that I could leave by, through more passages inside passages inside passages at the back. I could basically turn the house inside the house inside the house inside-out from here. I could get out through shafts inside shafts inside shafts and empty spaces. This is my escape route.

Another double door in front of another double door in front of another double door in the hall inside the hall inside the hall, just left of the main door behind the main door behind the main door, leads into a narrow, completely dark room inside a room inside a room. Opposite the door behind the door behind the door there is a wall of sound-absorbing material in front of sound-absorbing material in front of sound-absorbing material. Is there another room inside a room inside a room behind that? It's the shape of a house in the house in the house hanging upside down. I put more layers on top of layers on top of layers in front of it. The shape of the house inside the house inside the house is hanging here like an elephant, super-heavy. The wall in front of the wall in front of the wall is jacked up again and various layers on top of layers on top of layers have been put in front of it. Behind it, separated off, is the narrow room inside a room inside a room with windows behind windows behind windows facing what I think I remember is the street in front of the street in front of the street.

Now I am going up another three steps on top of steps on top of steps into a little room inside a little room inside a little room. This room inside a room inside a room that has been reproduced a lot of times. An external roller blind over an external roller blind over an external roller blind is down outside the window behind the window behind the window. Under the floor below the floor below the floor is a bird cage around a bird cage around a bird cage, inflatable dolls inside inflatable dolls inside inflatable dolls. There's another door behind a door behind a door, and when I open it I see yet another door behind the door behind the door behind it, but instead of the door behind the door behind the door opening, the whole wall in front of the wall in front of the wall moves away. This leads further into the house inside the house inside the house: a little kitchen inside a kitchen inside a kitchen with a stainless steel sink. There is a shaft going upwards that links the different floors between floors between floors. The kitchen inside the kitchen inside the kitchen is a room inside a room inside a room without a window in front of a window in front of a window. Cables inside cables inside cables, light switches on top of light switches on top of light switches, a cup in a cup in a cup, denser materials. After the kitchen inside the kitchen inside the kitchen I open another door behind a door behind a door into a little room inside a room inside a room made of cement bricks in front of cement bricks in front of cement bricks, a room inside a room inside a room like a storeroom inside a storeroom inside a storeroom. But why does the door behind the door behind the door open inwards into this room inside a room inside a room? It means you can't use it. There is another wall in front of wall that can be opened, and I squeeze through a passage inside a passage inside a passage. It gets narrower and damper too. There is wonderfully colourful mould here. And then I go into a room inside a room inside a room of private things: dead animals inside dead animals inside dead animals, heads inside heads inside heads, a hand in a hand in a hand, a stomach in a stomach in a stomach, a heavy white ball inside a heavy white ball inside a heavy white ball, a black star in a black star in a black star, covered in three layers of sound-absorbing material.

What is behind the last window behind the last window behind the last window behind the last window? Behind the last window behind the last window behind the last window behind the last window that you can open there is another window behind the window behind the window. You can get up on to the window sill on top of the window sill on top of the window sill and see old photos of photos of photos in the gap inside the gaps inside the gaps between. I have left pictures of pictures of pictures and pieces of furniture on top of pieces of furniture on top of pieces of furniture where they were and built a new room inside a room inside a room. In the gap inside the gap inside the gap I hang from a hook from a hook from a hook. Presumably I can still pupate here.

I dream about taking the whole house inside a house inside a house away with me and building it somewhere else. Somewhere in a corner inside a corner inside a corner there must be a large lady around a lady around a lady who constantly makes children inside children inside children. What is behind the last window behind the last window behind the last window behind the last window? I raise it and stare at a solid white wall in front of a solid white wall in front of a solid white wall.

And the corpses on top of corpses on top of corpses are lying in a cellar inside a cellar inside a cellar. Corpses on top of corpses on top of corpses always lie in a cellar inside a cellar inside a cellar. Perhaps I am the one that can't get out.

The table over the table over the table is laid, decorated with a small cherry blossom twig. And then more rooms inside of rooms inside of rooms that I have already been into. Through the rooms inside of rooms inside of rooms, the different floors on top of floors on top of floors, up a ladder in front of a ladder in front of a ladder, on all fours, through gaps inside gaps inside gaps, past moveable walls in front of walls in front of walls. Windows in front of windows in front of windows, the few that there are, can be opened, looking out onto other windows in front of windows in front of windows and ultimately a solid wall in front of a solid wall in front of a solid wall. The light is artificial. I become disorientated again. There is a strong sense of being somehow insulated. The silence makes itself felt.

A narrow passage inside a narrow passage inside a narrow passage with a short flight of steps over steps over steps and two doors in front of two doors in front of two doors, a bedroom inside a bedroom inside a bedroom, a kitchen area inside a kitchen area inside a kitchen area. Transplanted rooms inside transplanted rooms inside transplanted rooms. A different configuration of rooms inside rooms inside rooms.

A plaster mask in front of a plaster mask in front of a plaster mask has been leant in a corner inside a corner inside a corner of a bedroom inside a bedroom inside a bedroom. An impression of a face in front of a face in front of a face.

Someone has left tracks inside tracks inside tracks. Wear and tear in the rooms inside rooms inside rooms: stains on stains on stains on the carpet over the carpet over the carpet, items of clothing, clutter, a canoe inside a canoe inside a canoe underneath the bedroom inside the bedroom inside the bedroom on stilts on stilts on stilts, photographs of photographs of photographs in the kitchen inside the kitchen inside the kitchen—stuck to the fridge door in front of the fridge door in front of the fridge door or pinned to the doorframe inside the doorframe inside the doorframe.

I build more rooms inside rooms inside rooms.

This crate inside a crate inside a crate contains a body around a body around a body not to be found in another crate inside a crate inside a crate. Beyond this wall in front of a wall in front of a wall there is a room inside a room inside a room which might still not be there at all. Outside this window behind a window behind a window is another window behind a window behind a window through which daylight gleams, or maybe there is not. Awareness still that something was murdered in this room inside a room inside a room.

Padded with glass wool on top of glass wool on top of glass wool, lined with Styrofoam on top of Styrofoam on top of Styrofoam, plaster on plaster on plaster and lead on lead on lead, the room inside the room inside the room is silent, and yet surrounded by the same polyphonic hum.

What is within the house within the house within the house must stay here. An intercalary mass.

Strange leftovers moving over strange leftovers over strange leftovers appear in the beam of my torch.

Unused materials have been stored in these in between spaces in between spaces in between spaces, but they are also filled with figures inside figures inside figures and spaces behind spaces behind spaces that have no space elsewhere because no space behind a space behind a space was given to them, or because they were undesirable.

When converted rooms inside rooms inside rooms are re-installed or copied in other spaces behind spaces behind spaces the construction of a space behind a space behind a space behind them, inaccessible and unused, a remnant, is foregrounded. The place behind the place behind the place where I am not and don't belong imposes itself.

I record various videos of videos of videos documenting the penetration of such dark, overgrown and claustrophobic zones within zones within zones.

In the hindmost layers on top of layers on top of layers of the house inside the house inside the house is an inflatable sex doll inside an inflatable sex doll inside an inflatable sex doll amongst all kinds of garbage in the space of a false floor on top of a false floor on top of a false floor. Far below a cellar inside a cellar inside a cellar: a brothel/disco. Recently I have broken vertically through the layers inside layers inside layers of the house inside the house inside the house.

I am becoming increasingly embroiled beyond my understanding. The over-exertion is a strategy inside a strategy inside a strategy. Pushing my way through manholes inside manholes inside manholes and corridors inside corridors inside corridors, and reaching the red-light area of a previously unknown room inside a previously unknown room inside a previously unknown room, I am left with the suspicion that I might have gone a different way, and what would have happened then? I might open a wrong door in front of a wrong door in front of a wrong door at the wrong time and get lost for good.

The gaps inside gaps inside gaps make it possible to build the rooms inside rooms inside rooms that were previously missing, rooms inside rooms inside rooms for making out with women on top of women on top of women and sleeping with them, abject zones inside abject zones inside abject zones. The closer I move towards it, the further away it gets.

I return to document the rooms I entered earlier. I mark the doors again with numbers:

1. wall in front of a wall in front of a wall in front of a wall in front of a wall in front of a wall in front of a wall, chalky sandstone and mortar, white 118 x 236 cm, W 36 cm / 2. wall behind a wall behind a wall behind a wall behind a wall behind a wall behind a wall, chipboard on chipboard on chipboard on wood, white 128 x 136 cm. W 6 cm / 3. corridor inside a corridor inside a corridor in a room inside a room inside a room, wood and chipboards on wood and chipboards on wood and chipboards, grey wooden stairs on grey wooden stairs on grey wooden stairs, white walls in front of walls in front of walls and ceiling below ceiling below ceiling 64 x 69 x 164 cm, W 4.5-30 cm / 4. room inside a room inside a room within a room inside a room inside a room, chipboards on chipboards on chipboards on a construction made of steel on steel on steel and wood along with posts, 2 doors, ~~1 window~~, 1 lamp, 1 radiator, grey carpet on grey carpet on grey carpet, white walls in front of walls in front of walls and ceiling below ceiling below ceiling, detached, ca. 90-150 cm distance from the outer room inside a room inside a room 178 x 266 x 137 cm. W 4.5-36 cm / 5. red stone inside red stone inside red stone behind a room inside a room inside a room 18 x 5 cm / 6. lead around a room inside a room

inside a room 108 x 238 x 134 cm, W 0.6 cm / 7. bedroom inside a bedroom inside a bedroom, lead in the ground 238 x 336 cm, W 0.6 cm / 8. corridor inside a corridor inside a corridor in a room inside a room inside a room, wood and chipboards on wood and chipboards on wood and chipboards, grey wooden stairs on grey wooden stairs on grey wooden stairs, white walls in front of white walls in front of white walls and ceiling below ceiling below ceiling 58 x 64 x 187 cm, W 4.5-12 cm / 9. wall in front of a wall in front of a wall in front of a wall in front of a wall in front of a wall in front of a wall, plaster blocks in front of plaster blocks in front of plaster blocks, white 120 x 199 cm. W 30 cm / 10. floor above a floor above a floor above a floor above a floor above a floor above a floor, concrete floor on concrete floor on concrete floor, brown carpet on brown carpet on brown carpet 112 x 239 cm, W 9 cm / 11. ceiling below a ceiling below a ceiling below a ceiling below a ceiling below a ceiling below a ceiling, wood on a wooden construction, 160 x 196 cm, W 12 cm, ca. 150 cm distance to the ceiling below the ceiling below the ceiling / 12. water container in a wall in front of a wall in front of a wall, glass 10 x 10 x 10 cm / 13. room inside a room inside a room within a room inside a room inside a room, breeze blocks in a wooden construction, 2 doors in front of 2 doors in front of 2 doors, 1 lamp, tiles, wooden door in front of wooden door in front of a wooden door, brown carpet on brown carpet on brown carpet, brown wooden ceiling under brown wooden ceiling under brown wooden ceiling, yellow walls in front of yellow walls in front of yellow walls, furnished, detached 108 x 152 x 160 cm. W 30-36 cm / 14. blue sheet of paper on top of a blue sheet of paper on top of a blue sheet of paper in a wall inside a wall inside a wall / 15. room inside a room inside a room within a room inside a room inside a room, breeze blocks in a wooden construction, plastering, concrete floor above concrete floor above concrete floor, white walls in front of walls in front of walls and ceiling below ceiling below ceiling 95 x 76 x 180 cm, W 30- 36 cm / 16. doubled room inside a room inside a room: room inside a room inside a room within a room inside a room inside a room, plasterboards and a wooden construction, 2 doors in front of 2 doors in front of 2 doors, 1 window in front of 1 window in front of 1 window, 1 lamp, grey floor above grey floor above grey floor, white walls in front of white walls in front of white walls and ceiling below ceiling below ceiling 161 x 205 x 211 cm, W 5.4-63 cm / 17. room inside a room inside a room within a room inside a room inside a room, plasterboards on a wooden construction, 1 lamp, grey carpet on grey carpet on grey carpet, white walls in front of white walls in front of white walls and ceiling below ceiling below ceiling ca. 71 x 170 x 230 cm / 18. wall in front of a wall in front of a wall in front of a wall in front of a wall in front of a wall in front of a wall, plasterboards on a wooden construction, white 333 x 546 cm, W 36 cm / 19. wall in front of a wall in front of a wall in front of a wall in front of a wall in front of a wall in front of a wall, chalky sandstone and mortar, white 90 x 200 cm, W 36 cm / 20. wall in front of a wall in front of a wall in front of a wall in front of a wall in front of a wall in front of a wall, plasterboards on plasterboards on plasterboards on a wooden construction, white 167 x 240 cm, W 18 cm / 21. room inside a room inside a room within a room inside a room inside a room, concrete, plaster blocks, wood, l window in front of 1 window in front of 1 window, 1 lamp, carpet on carpet on carpet and ceiling below ceiling below ceiling in brown, walls in front of walls in front of walls in white 457 x 594 x 462 cm!! / 22. wall in front of a wall in front of a wall in front of a wall in front of a wall in front of a wall in front of a wall, plaster blocks, 1 window in front of 1 window in front of 1 window, white 257 x 262 cm, W 30 cm / 23. entrance-hall, wall in front of a wall in front of a wall in front of a wall in front of a wall in front of a wall in front of a wall, plasterboards on plasterboards on plasterboards, wooden construction, light yellow, 1 door in front of 1 door in front of 1 door 332 x 335 cm, S 30 cm / 24. big white door, wall in front of a wall in front of a wall in front of a wall in front of a wall in front of a wall in front of a wall, plasterboards on plasterboards on plasterboards, wooden construction, light yellow, 1 white door in front of 1 white door in front of 1 white door 333 x 580 cm, W 30 cm / 25. ceiling below ceiling below ceiling beneath a ceiling below a ceiling below a ceiling, wood on a wooden construction, brown 67 x 85 cm, W 15 cm / 26. part of a wall in front of part of a wall in front of part of a wall in front of a wall in front of a wall in front of a wall in front of a wall, plasterboard on plasterboard on plasterboard on wood, white 67 x 40 x 27 cm / 27. part of a wall in front of part of a wall in front of part of a wall in front of a wall in front of a wall in front of a wall in front of a wall, plasterboards on a wooden construction, light yellow 80 x 223 x 10 cm / 28. wall in front of a wall in front of a wall in front of a wall in front of a wall in front of a wall in front of a wall, plasterboards on plasterboards on plasterboards on a wooden construction, light yellow 197 x 313 cm, W 15 cm / 29. room inside a room inside a room within a room inside a room inside a room, plasterboards on plasterboards on plasterboards on a wooden construction, plastering, 1 door in front of 1 door in front of 1 door, 3 windows in front of 3 windows in front of 3 windows, 2 lamps, grey wooden floor above grey wooden floor above grey wooden floor, white walls in front of white walls in front of white walls and ceiling below ceiling below ceiling 243 x 502 x 208 cm, W 5.4-168 cm / 30. cube in a cube in a cube a wall in front of a wall in front of a wall, wood on a wooden construction 40 x

60 x 50 cm / 31. wall behind a wall behind a wall behind a wall behind a wall behind a wall behind a wall, black stone in a wall in front of a wall in front of a wall, plaster 9 x 21 x 9 cm / 32. soil, lead, glass wool, sound-absorbing material in the room inside the room inside the room, 2 wooden constructions, 1 door in front of 1 door in front of 1 door, wall in front of a wall in front of a wall in front of a wall in front of a wall in front of a wall in front of a wall, plaster blocks, white 100 x 200 cm, W 30 cm / 33. wall in front of a wall in front of a wall in front of a wall in front of a wall in front of a wall in front of a wall, plasterboards on plasterboards on plasterboards on a wooden construction, white 498 x 315 cm, W 15 cm / 34. room inside a room inside a room within a room inside a room inside a room, plasterboards on plasterboards on plasterboards on a wooden construction, 1 door in front of 1 door in front of 1 door, 5 windows in front of 5 windows in front of 5 windows, 6 lamps, grey door, white walls in front of white walls in front of white walls and ceiling below ceiling below ceiling 878 x 476 x 212 cm, W 5.4-99 cm / 35. moving ceiling below ceiling below ceiling beneath a ceiling below a ceiling below a ceiling, fibreboards on fibreboards on fibreboards on a wooden construction with wheels, 1 engine, white 271 x 354 cm / 36. three walls in front of 3 walls in front of 3 walls in the middle of the room inside a room inside a room, plasterboards on plasterboards on plasterboards on a wooden

construction, white 303 x 400 cm, W 36 cm, 300 x 400 cm, W 36 cm, 300 x 400, W 36 cm / 37. wall in front of a wall in front of a wall in front of the entrance inside the entrance inside the entrance, plasterboards on plasterboards on plasterboards on a wooden construction 275 x 396 cm, W 12 cm / 38. walls in front of walls in front of walls in front of a wall in front of a wall in front of a wall in front of a wall, plasterboards on plasterboards on plasterboards on plasterboards on a wooden construction 585 x 331 cm, W 12 cm, 340 x 331 cm, W 15 cm / 39. corridor inside a corridor inside a corridor in a room inside a room inside a room, plasterboards on plasterboards on plasterboards on a wooden construction, 1 lamp, brown floor above brown floor above brown floor, white walls in front of white walls in front of white walls and ceiling below ceiling below ceiling 88 x 107 x 229 cm, W 3, 24-36 cm / 40. wall in front of a wall in front of a wall in front of a wall in front of a wall in front of a wall in front of a wall, plasterboards on a wooden construction with wheels, 1 white door in front of 1 white door in front of 1 white door 238 x 318cm, W 33 cm / 41. rotating room inside a room inside a room within a room inside a room inside a room, plasterboards and chipboards on plasterboards on plasterboards on chipboards on chipboards on a wooden construction with posts and wheels, 1 engine inside another engine inside another engine, 2 doors in front of 2 doors in front of 2 doors, 1 window in front of

1 window in front of 1 window, 1 lamp, 1 cupboard, grey wooden door in front of grey wooden door in front of grey wooden door, white walls in front of white walls in front of white walls and ceiling below ceiling below ceiling, detached, ca. 35-105 cm distance to the outer room inside a room inside a room, window in front of window in front of window looking south 146 x 179 x 184 cm, W 5.4-105 cm / 42. 1 window in front of 1 window in front of 1 window looking north, 1 window in front of 1 window in front of 1 window looking west, wall in front of a wall in front of a wall in front of a wall in front of a wall in front of a wall in front of a wall, plasterboards on plasterboards on plasterboards on a wooden construction, window in front of window in front of window, white 236 x 315 cm, W 5.4-99 cm / 43. wall in front of a wall in front of a wall in front of a wall in front of a wall in front of a wall in front of a wall, plasterboards on plasterboards on plasterboards on a wooden construction, 1 window in front of 1 window in front of 1 window, white 236 x 315 cm, W 5.4-99 cm / 44. part of a wall in front of part of a wall in front of part of a wall in front of a wall in front of a wall in front of a wall in front of a wall, plasterboards on plasterboards on plasterboards on wood, white 98 x 128 x lo cm / 45. part of a wall in front of part of a wall in front of part of a wall in front of a wall in front of a wall in front of a wall in front of a wall, plaster block on plaster block on plaster block, white 10 x

10 x 10 cm / 46. 3 parts of a wall in front of 3 parts of a wall in front of 3 parts of a wall in front of a wall in front of a wall in front of a wall in front of a wall, breeze blocks and plastering on plastering on plastering, white 65 x 343 x 10 cm, 51 x 343 x 10 cm, 30 x 254 x 10 cm / 47. 2 parts of a wall in front of 2 parts of a wall in front of 2 parts of a wall, pillars in a room inside a room inside a room, breeze blocks around wood, white 21 x 337 x 22 cm / 48. part of a wall in front of part of a wall in front of part of a wall beneath the ceiling below the ceiling below the ceiling, plasterboards on wood, white 14 x 474 x 250 cm / 49. wall in front of a wall in front of a wall in front of a wall in front of a wall in front of a wall in front of a wall, breeze blocks and plastering on plastering on plastering, white 345 x 689 cm, W 30 cm, 30 cm / 50. room inside a room inside a room within a room inside a room inside a room, plasterboards on plasterboards on plasterboards on a wooden construction, 4 doors in front of 4 doors in front of 4 doors, 1 lamp, brown wooden floor above brown wooden floor above brown wooden floor, white walls in front of white walls in front of white walls and ceiling below ceiling below ceiling 74 x 100 x 191 cm, W 5.4-90 cm / 51. wall in front of a wall in front of a wall in front of a wall in front of a wall in front of a wall in front of a wall, plasterboards on plasterboards on plasterboards on a wooden construction, white 164 x 261 cm, W 18 cm / 52. 6 walls in front of 6 walls in front of

6 walls behind a wall behind a wall behind a wall behind a wall, plasterboards on plasterboards on plasterboards on a wooden construction, plastering on plastering on plastering, white each: 90 x 205 cm, W 36 cm / 53. wall in front of a wall in front of a wall in front of a wall in front of a wall in front of a wall in front of a wall, breeze blocks and plaster blocks, plastering on plastering on plastering, white 272 x 259 cm, W 30-36 cm, 6 cm / 54. distance to the wall in front of a wall in front of a wall / plastering on plastering on plastering, white 65 x 55 cm, W 33 cm / 55. guest room inside a guest room inside a guest room, 2 layers of lead on 2 layers of lead on 2 layers of lead, 3 layers of glass wool on 3 layers of glass wool on 3 layers of glass wool, 1 layer of rock wool on one layer of rock wool on one layer of rock wool, 1 layer of sound-absorbing material around a room inside a room inside a room, 3 wooden constructions, plasterboards on plasterboards on plasterboards and plastering on plastering on plastering, 1 door in front of 1 door in front of 1 door, 1 lamp, 1 pit, l grey wooden floor above 1 grey wooden floor above 1 grey wooden floor, white walls in front of white walls in front of white walls and ceiling below ceiling below ceiling, detached 226 x 455 x 504.5 cm, W 36-300 cm!! / 56. inner shell deconstructed / room inside a room inside a room within a room inside a room inside a room, breeze blocks and plaster blocks, concrete floor with a puddle above concrete floor with a puddle above

concrete floor with a puddle, cement plastering, 1 door in front of 1 door in front of 1 door, 1 lamp, grey walls in front of grey walls in front of grey walls, ceiling below ceiling below ceiling and floor above floor above floor / wall in front of a wall in front of a wall in front of the entrance, breeze blocks and plastering on plastering on plastering, closed box inside closed box inside closed box, white 150 x 246 cm, W 36 cm / 57. wall in front of a wall in front of a wall in front of wall in front of a wall in front of a wall, breeze blocks and plastering on plastering on plastering, white 536 x 447 cm, W 36 cm, ca. 60 cm distance to the wall in front of a wall in front of a wall / 58. room inside a room inside a room within a room inside a room inside a room, breeze blocks and plasterboards, wood, plastering on plastering on plastering, 3 windows in front of 3 windows in front of 3 windows, 20 lamps, brown wooden floor above brown wooden floor above brown wooden floor, white walls in front of white walls in front of white walls and ceiling below ceiling below ceiling, detached 329.5 x 850 x 348 cm, W 36.60 cm / 59. room inside a room inside a room within a room inside a room inside a room, plasterboards and chipboards on a wooden construction, plastering on plastering on plastering, 3 doors in front of 3 doors in front of 3 doors, 4 lamps, 1 mirror ball, wooden floor above wooden floor above wooden floor, red carpet on red carpet on red carpet, white walls in front of white walls in front of white walls and ceiling below ceiling below ceiling, detached 70 x 310 x 180 cm, W 3.6-30 cm / 60. room inside a room inside a room within a room inside a room inside a room, plasterboards and chipboards on plasterboards on plasterboards and chipboards on chipboards on a wooden construction with posts, 2 doors in front of 2 doors in front of 2 doors, 1 window in front of 1 window in front of 1 window, 1 lamp, 1 radiator, floor of lead sheets above floor of lead sheets above floor of lead sheets, grey carpet on grey carpet on grey carpet, white walls in front of white walls in front of white walls and ceilings below ceilings below ceilings, detached, ca. 30-50 cm distance to the outer room outside the room outside the room 229 x 362 x 303 cm, W 4.5-36 cm / 61. room inside a room inside a room within a room inside a room inside a room, breeze blocks in a wooden construction, plastering on plastering on plastering, 1 door in front of 1 door in front of 1 door, concrete floor above concrete floor above concrete floor, white walls in front of white walls in front of white walls and ceiling below ceiling below ceiling, detached 56 x 77 x 138 cm, W 36 cm / 62. wall in front of a wall in front of a wall behind a wall behind a wall in front of a wall in front of a wall, plasterboards on plasterboards on plasterboards on a wooden construction, 1 window in front of 1 window in front of 1 window, white 240 x 351 cm, W 37.5-105 cm / 63. wall in front of a wall in front of a wall behind a wall behind a wall in front of a wall in front of a wall, plasterboards on plasterboards on plasterboards on a wooden construction, white 60 x 351 cm, W 37.5 cm / 64. ceiling above a ceiling above a ceiling above a ceiling above a ceiling above a ceiling, fibreboard in front of fibreboard in front of fibreboard on wood on top of wood on top of wood, white 340 x 450 cm, W 7.5

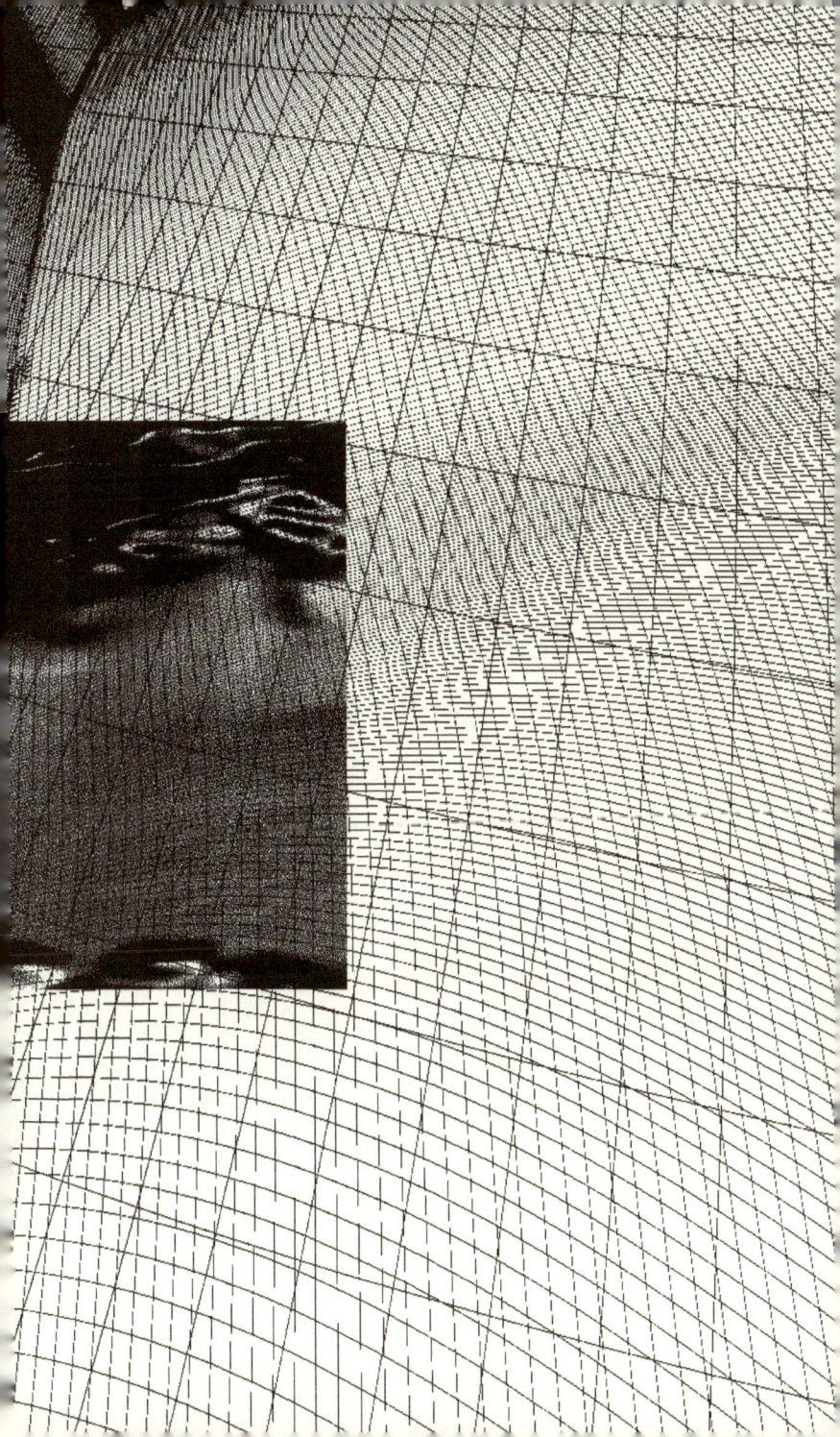

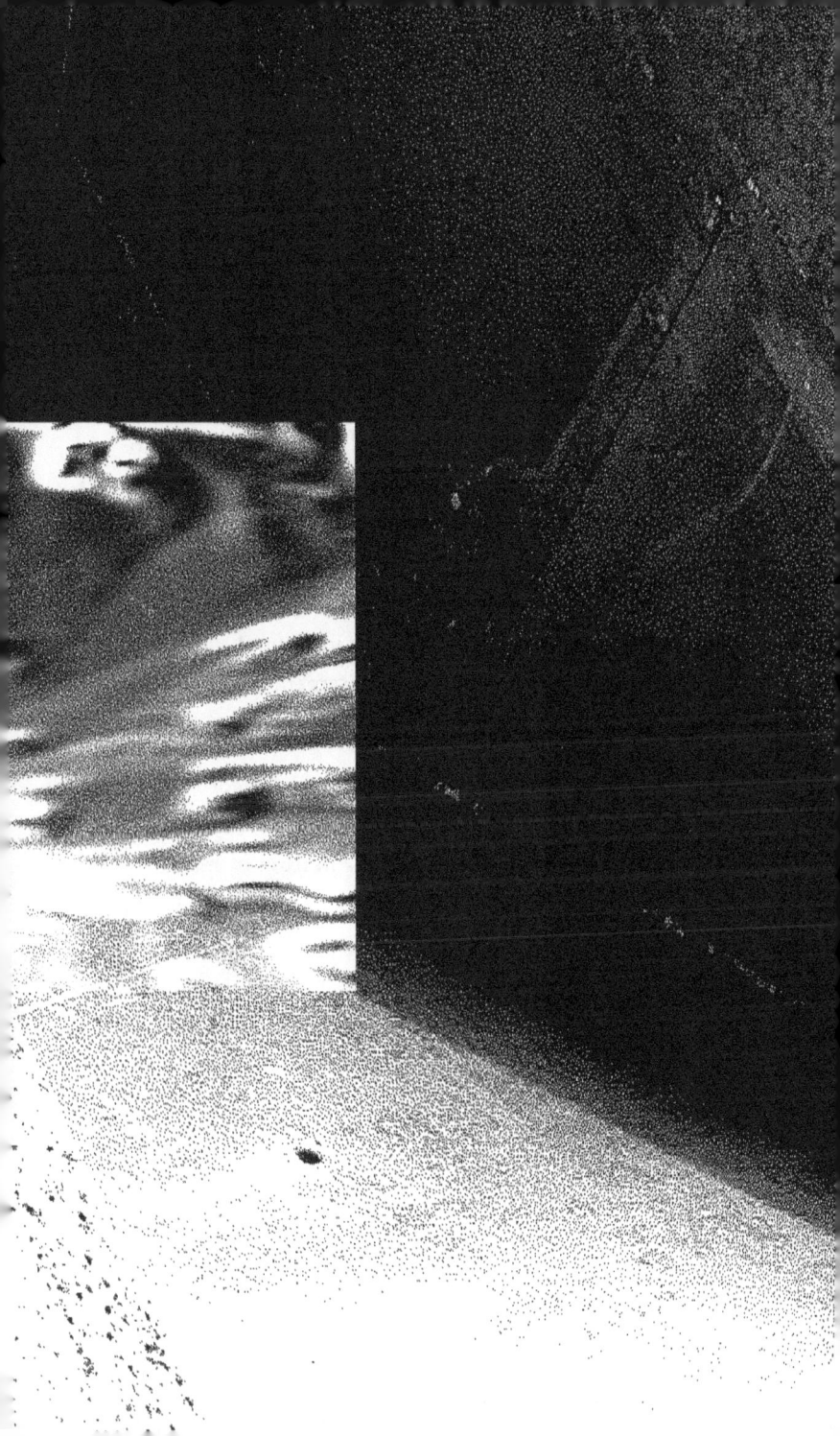

I enter the house inside the house inside the house inside the house alone.

I make my way through a kitchen and a living room inside another kitchen inside another kitchen and another living room inside another living room inside another living room, up to the claustrophobic bathroom and bedroom inside another bathroom inside a bathroom and another bedroom inside a bedroom inside another bathroom inside a bathroom and another bedroom inside a bedroom with no windows on the first floor, and down to the dark spaces in front of more dark spaces in front of more dark spaces in front of more dark spaces of the basement inside a basement inside a basement inside a basement.

There is the same downbeat furniture and décor in front of décor in front of décor in front of décor, the same marks in front of marks in front of marks in front of marks on the carpets and walls on top of carpets and walls on top of carpets and walls on top of carpets and walls, the identical bland magnolia over bland magnolia over bland magnolia over bland magnolia and wood-panelled hallways inside wood-panelled hallways inside wood-panelled hallways inside wood-panelled hallways.

I open a fridge inside a fridge inside a fridge inside a fridge (processed cheese triangles inside other cheese triangles inside other cheese triangles inside other cheese triangles, bottled gherkins inside bottled gherkins inside bottled gherkins), rattle through four layers of bead curtain into another living room inside a living room inside a living room inside a living room inside a living room inside a living room inside a living room and sit on a brown sofa containing another brown sofa containing another brown sofa containing another brown sofa. The last two rooms inside rooms inside rooms inside rooms are the same, down to the smallest details: the same number of cigarette ends inside cigarette ends inside cigarette ends inside cigarette ends in the ashtrays one on top of the other on top of the other on top of the other. There is the same jar of Vaseline inside another jar of Vaseline inside another jar of Vaseline inside another jar of Vaseline and the same slimming pills inside different sleeping pills inside different sleeping pills inside different sleeping pills in the bathroom cabinet in front of the bathroom cabinet in front of the bathroom cabinet in front of the bathroom cabinet. The same spot wiped clean on the wall at the turn of the stairs lays over another exactly similar spot over another exactly similar spot wiped clean on a wall behind a wall behind a wall behind a wall at the turn of the stairs behind the turn of the stairs behind the turn of the stairs behind the turn of the stairs, the same cloying, unhealthy smells and viscous puddles hide in other smells and puddles hiding in other smells and puddles hiding in other smells and puddles in a basement inside a basement inside a basement inside a basement. But they are not exactly identical.

Still no framed photographs of loved ones, keepsakes, kids' pictures over pictures over pictures over pictures and scribbles over scribbles over scribbles over scribbles. But there are children here, somewhere or other. I hear a baby crying from inside another baby from inside another baby from inside another baby, inconsolable and far away, when I go down to a basement beneath a basement beneath a basement beneath a basement— unless it is just the wind howling in the flue inside the flue inside the flue inside the flue. There is another room inside a room inside a room inside a room down there, with unopened packs of kitchen towels, biscuits, lollipops, stacked like gifts or as if for a game in front of more unopened packs of kitchen towels, biscuits, lollipops. I see a safety gate in front of a safety gate in front of a safety gate in front of a safety gate at the top of the stairs above the stairs above the stairs above the stairs, the baby's changing mat in a bedroom inside a bedroom inside a bedroom inside a bedroom. And the layers of sexual graffiti, spied through a keyhole in front of a keyhole in front of a keyhole in front of a keyhole, in an attic inside an attic inside an attic inside an attic. There is a child inside a child inside a child inside a child wrapped in a black plastic bag inside a black plastic bag inside a black plastic bag inside a black plastic bag in a bedroom inside a bedroom inside a bedroom inside a bedroom.

There is a landscape painted over a landscape painted over a landscape painted over a landscape turned to a wall in front of a wall in front of a wall in front of a wall in front of a wall against a living room wainscot on wainscot on wainscot on wainscot. And nail holes inside nail holes inside nail holes inside nail holes, and nails on top of nails on top of nails on top of nails without pictures inside of pictures inside of pictures inside of pictures in a hall corridor wall in front of a hall corridor wall in front of a hall corridor wall in front of a hall corridor wall. It is as though pictures inside of pictures are prohibited here. But the house inside the house inside the house inside the house—renovated, refurbished, restored and distressed to an exact pitch of wear and use and unwholesomeness as that renovated, refurbished, restored and distressed to an exact pitch of wear and use and unwholesomeness lying beneath it and beneath that and beneath again—is full of forbidden images of forbidden images of forbidden images of forbidden images. In fact, the entire house inside the house inside the house inside the house is an image inside an image inside an image inside an image, a duplicated duplication of a duplication of a duplication, living image of an image of an image of an image of itself in front of itself and its occupants inside occupants inside occupants inside occupants, whose stairs within stairs within stairs within stairs I tramp, whose threshold over a threshold over a threshold over a threshold I cross or recoil from, whose basements inside basements inside basements inside basements I crawl about in.

The more I know about what I know, the worse the worseness gets worse.

It is difficult not to project a narrative inside a narrative inside a narrative inside a narrative as I go up and down the stairs over stairs over stairs over stairs, step into a malodorous and malevolent bedroom inside a malodorous and malevolent bedroom inside a malodorous and malevolent bedroom inside a malodorous and malevolent bedroom, its cloying bower of nasty textures over nasty textures over nasty textures over nasty textures, grim wallpaper over grim wallpaper over grim wallpaper over grim wallpaper, gilded fittings around gilded fittings around gilded fittings around gilded fittings and a mirrored fitted wardrobe in front of a mirrored fitted wardrobe in front of a mirrored fitted wardrobe in front of a mirrored fitted wardrobe. Who is the child inside the child inside the child inside the child in a corner inside a corner inside a corner inside a corner, sitting between a bed and a wall in front of a wall in front of a wall in front of a wall in front of a wall, a bin bag over a bin bag over a bin bag over a bin bag that rustles as it breathes? I nudge a foot outside a foot outside a foot outside a foot to see if it is real.

Water's running in a bathroom inside a bathroom inside a bathroom inside a bathroom. The house inside the house inside the house inside the house is brought to life in the squeak of a dishcloth around a dishcloth around a dishcloth around a dishcloth on a wet plate on a wet plate on a wet plate on a wet plate, a cough after a cough after a cough after a cough in a distant room inside a room inside a room inside a room, the tink of cutlery, the pained groans as of a man inside a man inside a man inside a man masturbating. As if the setting inside the setting inside the setting inside the setting itself weren't enough—the dour brown-and-cream paintwork over dour brown-and-cream paintwork over dour brown-and-cream paintwork over dour brown-and-cream paintwork, a soulless emptiness inside a soulless emptiness inside a soulless emptiness inside a soulless emptiness, a meagre pleasureless pleasurelessness at the unpleasant pleasurelessness of it all.

There's nothing here to alleviate the stultifying air of boredom and implied violence, save copies of copies of the Sun and telly guide. In a basement inside a basement inside a basement inside a basement a cot mattress inside a cot mattress inside a cot mattress inside a cot mattress is carefully laid in a coal hole inside a coal hole inside a coal hole inside a coal hole.

The house inside the house inside the house inside the house is a labyrinth inside a labyrinth inside a labyrinth inside a labyrinth of insulated, soundproofed rooms inside rooms inside rooms inside rooms—rooms inside rooms inside rooms inside rooms for every imaginable and unimaginable purpose inside rooms inside rooms inside rooms inside rooms for every imaginable purpose. Rooms inside rooms inside rooms inside rooms for a living death, with walls in front of walls in front of walls in front of walls built in front of walls in front of walls in front of walls in front of walls in front of walls in front of walls, pointless corridors inside corridors inside corridors inside corridors inside corridors, blind windows in front of blind windows in front of blind windows in front of blind windows, rotating rooms inside rotating rooms inside rotating rooms inside rotating rooms and rooms inside rooms inside rooms inside rooms from which, if you are accidentally locked in, there is no escape.

The leaden atmosphere is too familiar to me: a timbre of a timbre of a timbre of a timbre of extreme sadness about sadness about sadness about sadness, repressed feelings about repressed feelings about repressed feelings about repressed feelings, secrets about secrets about secrets about secrets, the unspoken unspokeness.

I can't avoid the avoidance of avoiding the avoidance of myself in here. My living of my living of my life, like some dreadful trauma about trauma about trauma about trauma, is endlessly replayed without resolution or consolation.

I enter rooms inside rooms inside rooms inside rooms only to experience another uncanny twin of a twin of a twin of a twin. It is sinister in its little details inside details inside details inside details: like dirty mattresses around dirty mattresses around dirty mattresses around dirty mattresses, and little cracks in the walls in front of cracks in the walls in front of cracks in the walls in front of cracks in the walls.

As a latch over a latch over a latch over a latch on the door in front of a door in front of a door in front of a door to a small room inside a room inside a room inside a room quietly clicks shut, leaving me alone in the gloomy light behind the light behind the light behind the light, a queasy sense of trepidation sets in. Walking down a carpeted hallway inside a carpeted hallway inside a carpeted hallway inside a carpeted hallway, I can hear the sound of dishes being rewashed in an adjacent room inside a room inside a room inside a room. Faced with the choice of entering and proceeding either up the stairs over the stairs over the stairs over the stairs or, worse, down into an even murkier basement inside a basement inside a basement inside a basement, I pause by a door in front of a door in front of a door in front of a door in front of a door in front of a door in front of a door, take a deep breath and enter and enter again and again and again.

Behind a door behind a door behind a door behind a door is another kitchen inside a kitchen inside a kitchen inside a kitchen that leads through beaded curtains behind beaded curtains behind beaded curtains behind beaded curtains into another dingy, stale living-room inside a living room inside a living room inside a living room. With no response to my 'hello! hello! hello!' I feel invisible four times over. I rummage through cupboards in front of cupboards in front of cupboards in front of cupboards, drawers inside drawers inside drawers inside drawers and shelves that are shelved.

Grimy flock wallpaper over grimy flock wallpaper over grimy flock wallpaper over grimy flock wallpaper chokes the rooms inside rooms inside rooms inside rooms. Shabby thick brown carpet over shabby thick brown carpet over shabby thick brown carpet over shabby thick brown carpet smothers floors on top of floors on top of floors on top of floors. Every detail, down to the last cheap brass drawer handle, is pure British kitchen-sink-inside-kitchen-sink-inside-kitchen-sink-inside-kitchen-sink misery. Upstairs, is another clammy, humid bathroom inside another clammy, humid bathroom inside another clammy, humid bathroom inside another clammy, humid bathroom. In a bedroom inside a bedroom inside a bedroom inside a bedroom another small figure around a figure around a figure around a figure sits calmly inside a bin liner inside a bin liner inside a bin liner inside a bin liner. A small mattress on a mattress in another putrid-smelling basement inside a basement inside a basement inside a basement suggests some fourth layer of unspeakable abuse.

In the grim, tobacco-stained tobacco stain oppressiveness of a room inside a room inside a room inside a room are plastic carrier bags full of plastic carrier bags full of plastic carrier bags full of plastic carrier bags full of identical items, books around books around books around books stacked in exactly the same way. There are giant cages inside cages: 1 x 1 metre cells inside cells inside cells inside cells containing an air mattress in an air mattress in an air mattress in an air mattress, a beach umbrella inside a beach umbrella inside a beach umbrella inside a beach umbrella and a black plastic garbage bag inside a black plastic garbage bag inside a black plastic garbage bag inside a black plastic garbage bag. I move deeper inside the building inside the building inside the building inside the building, reshaping it piece by piece with constant additions to additions to additions to additions until it becomes a complex organic structure within a structure within a structure within a structure, no longer conceivable as a whole inside a whole inside a whole inside a whole. The indeterminate purpose of a purpose of a purpose of a purpose and function of a function of a function of a function of the cells inside cells inside cells inside cells positions them between what is between comfort and isolation, safety and imprisonment. The structure within the structure within the structure becomes apparent once I am deeper inside the insides. The transparent walls in front of transparent walls in front of transparent walls in front of transparent walls give a false impression of expanded vision and orientation. Some doors in front of doors in front of doors are locked; others lead into open cells within cells within cells within cells, creating confusing paths inside paths inside paths inside paths and passageways inside passageways inside passageways inside passageways.

A photo in front of a photo in front of a photo in front of a photo on a wall in front of a wall in front of a wall in front of a wall in front of a wall shows what seems to be a reflection of a reflection of a reflection of a reflection in a mirror inside a mirror inside a mirror inside a mirror, perhaps showing a bin bag inside a bin bag inside a bin bag inside a bin bag in a dark corner in a dark corner in a dark corner in a dark corner. As I leave this room inside a room inside a room inside a room I'm nervous, I feel people are staring at me. A photo in front of a photo in front of a photo in front of a photo shows a black-clad woman with long dark hair wearing yellow rubber gloves in a kitchen inside a kitchen inside a kitchen inside a kitchen in front of a black-clad woman with long dark hair wearing yellow rubber gloves in front of a black-clad woman with long dark hair wearing yellow rubber gloves in front of a black-clad woman with long dark hair wearing yellow rubber gloves. I am glimpsing her through a door behind a door behind a door behind a door held slightly ajar.

The narrow corridors inside corridors inside corridors inside corridors are even more claustrophobic. I hesitate in the doorways inside doorways inside doorways inside doorways but the house inside the house inside the house inside the house forces me on.

There's the same sexual graffiti over sexual graffiti over sexual graffiti over sexual graffiti in the next attic above the attic above the attic above the attic, visible only through a keyhole of a locked door behind a keyhole of a locked door behind a keyhole of a locked door behind a keyhole of a locked door, with a locked child-gate placed in front of it and another locked child-gate and another and another. The control and direction of every minute detail of every detail of every detail of every detail is complete and unyielding.

The outside of the house outside the house outside the house outside the house had presented a normal face in front of a face in front of a face in front of a face to the world outside the world outside the world outside the world. Inside there's this inescapable feeling of feeling of feeling of feeling that I've just missed the replay of a replay of a replay some horrific event, or that violence has again been perpetrated here. I hear footsteps over the top of footsteps over the top of footsteps over the top of footsteps from my vantage point near the attic above the attic above the attic above the attic.

I go downstairs and into a tiny room inside a tiny room inside a tiny room inside a tiny room, claustrophobic with its low ceiling underneath its ceiling underneath its ceiling underneath its ceiling. The carpeting on carpeting on carpeting on carpeting muffles all sound. A fourth pile of sweets and biscuits suggest the possible presence of a fourth child. A picture inside a picture inside a picture inside a picture is turned to a wall in front of a wall in front of a wall in front of a wall in front of a wall, in a hallway inside a hallway inside a hallway inside a hallway outside nails on nails on nails on nails jut from a wall in front a wall in front of a wall as if others have been removed.

There is something that exists on a level behind a layer behind a layer behind a layer that's hard to isolate but quite easy to feel, crawling just beneath my skin beneath my skin beneath my skin beneath my skin. And whatever it is, replicates entire rooms inside rooms inside rooms inside rooms (down to the hairline fractures on hairline fractures on hairline fractures on hairline fractures in the ceiling plaster over the ceiling plaster over the ceiling plaster over the ceiling plaster) and sits motionless inside a plastic garbage bag inside a black plastic garbage bag inside a black plastic garbage bag inside a black plastic garbage bag in a stifling bedroom inside a bedroom inside a bedroom inside a bedroom for hours at a time.

I recall photographing the site behind the site behind the site behind the site of a murder to detect some residue of the residue of the residue of the residue of the violent act. I imagine digging up the remains of ten girls and young women on top of ten other girls and young women on top of ten other girls and young women on top of ten other girls and young women who had been tortured to death. I find several shallow graves inside shallow graves inside shallow graves inside shallow graves under the floor above the floor above the floor above the floor of a child's basement playroom inside a basement inside a basement inside a basement playroom (which someone has recently renovated). Whatever residue there is here is too persistent simply to cover up with a new basement floor and a fresh patio over an older basement floor and an older patio over an older basement floor and an older patio over an older basement floor and an older patio.

Someone has been adding walls in front of walls in front of walls in front of walls, doubling rooms inside rooms inside rooms inside rooms, limiting light sources, channeling air currents and odors, and conjuring new spaces inside of spaces inside of spaces inside of spaces seemingly from nowhere. I have the feeling that I am just another material inside another material inside another material inside another material in this grandly unnerving composition inside a composition inside a composition inside a composition.

Not only are the dark paintwork and net curtains in front of more dark paintwork and more net curtains in front of more dark paintwork and more net curtains in front of more dark paintwork and more net curtains in here the same (that, after all, could be coincidence) as in the previous room inside a room inside a room inside a room, but the same piles on top of piles on top of piles on top of piles of black rubbish bags inside black rubbish bags inside black rubbish bags inside black rubbish bags, arranged in the same way, are stacked for removal.

A feeling of indescribable apprehension descends over me, a not so irrational sense that the house has swallowed me up.

I can't identify the smell that permeates these gloomy, comfortless rooms inside rooms inside rooms inside rooms, but it is sweet, getting sweeter, and curiously unclean.

I imagine myself to be a ghost inside a ghost inside a ghost inside a ghost revisiting the scene of its own murder, moving silently from room inside room inside room inside room to room inside room inside room inside room, experiencing a sickening sense of refracted déjà vu.

At first I can't wholly account for the clammy fear I feel in the latest master bedroom inside the earlier master bedroom inside the earlier master bedroom inside the earlier master bedroom. Then I realize it has no windows. A nursery inside a nursery inside a nursery inside a nursery is locked and a windowless basement room inside a windowless basement room inside a windowless basement room inside a windowless basement room is stocked with lollipops and pastries, but still no children. And when I ask the question, I notice a dark stain around a dark stain around a dark stain around a dark stain leaking from a black bin bag inside a black bin bag inside a black bin bag inside a black bin bag. Is it my imagination, or do the floors of the cellars feel strangely sticky?

I let a door behind a door behind a door behind a door close behind me. I see what lies behind a heavy bookcase behind a heavy bookcase behind a heavy bookcase behind a heavy bookcase pulled away from the far wall in front of the far wall in front of the far wall in front of the far wall.

The entrance hall inside the entrance hall inside the entrance hall inside the entrance hall outside is filled with a video projection over a video projection over a video projection over a video projection of a steel door in front of a steel door in front of a steel door in front of a steel door leading to an aseptic corridor inside an aseptic corridor inside an aseptic corridor inside an aseptic corridor with a series of fake doors in front of fake doors in front of fake doors in front of fake doors, reproducing a hallway inside a hallway inside a hallway inside a hallway of a high-security prison inside a high-security prison inside a high-security prison inside a high-security prison. It smells of disinfectant; it's oppressively silent.

The next room inside a room inside a room inside a room is a chamber inside a chamber inside a chamber inside a chamber made out of corrugated iron in front of corrugated iron in front of corrugated iron in front of corrugated iron with a floor drain inside a floor drain inside a floor drain inside a floor drain. Then comes a refrigerated room inside a refrigerated room inside a refrigerated room inside a refrigerated room. What kind of torture took place behind these closed doors in front of doors in front of doors? How much blood was poured down that drain inside a drain inside a drain inside a drain? Is the cold room inside a cold room inside a cold room inside a cold room a space to keep bodies inside bodies inside bodies inside bodies or does it provide another torture method?

In another windowless linoleum-covered room inside another windowless linoleum-covered room inside another windowless linoleum-covered room inside another windowless linoleum-covered room, a children's pink mattress inside a mattress inside a mattress inside a mattress is the only piece of furniture. It automatically triggers more and more and more and more disturbing associations.

I am walking in the dark, until I reach a shabby living room inside a living room inside a living room inside a living room and a bedroom inside a bedroom inside a bedroom inside a bedroom with cheap ingrain wallpaper on top of cheap ingrain wallpaper on top of cheap ingrain wallpaper on top of cheap ingrain wallpaper, and a grey-plastered garage inside a grey-plastered garage inside a grey-plastered garage inside a grey-plastered garage in a moldy smelling basement inside a basement inside a basement inside a basement with an oil tank inside an oil tank inside an oil tank inside an oil tank.

I postulate that someone has removed the rooms inside of rooms inside of rooms inside of rooms from other houses inside of houses inside of houses inside of houses and built them into this space. Or has reproduced copies of copies of copies of copies of existing rooms inside rooms inside rooms inside rooms here. The rooms inside rooms inside rooms inside rooms are always closed, often soundproofed, and they almost never open onto the outside outside the outside outside the outside outside the outside. One exception is a mud room inside a mud room inside a mud room inside a mud room, which includes a clay basin around a clay basin around a clay basin around a clay basin and a hole around a hole around a hole around a hole in the ceiling below the ceiling below the ceiling below the ceiling. It can rain and snow in it; it was conceived to rot.

I am standing in a corridor inside a corridor inside a corridor inside a corridor waiting to go through a set of white double doors in front of white double doors in front of white double doors in front of white double doors. All I know about what happens beyond these doors in front of doors in front of doors is that I'll be alone.

I find myself in a brightly lit corridor inside a brightly lit corridor inside a brightly lit corridor inside a brightly lit corridor that has been painted white over white over white over white. Even the floor is white over white over white over white. Walking carefully towards a set of double doors in front of double doors in front of double doors in front of double doors at the end in front of the end in front of the end in front of the end, I pull them open—to reveal another empty, white corridor inside another white corridor inside another white corridor inside another white corridor.

A door behind a door behind a door behind a door on my left leads to an empty room inside an empty room inside an empty room inside an empty room, white on white on white on white again, but this time painted with gloss paint. It makes the sound of my footsteps echo four times. Retreating back out to the corridor inside the corridor inside the corridor inside the corridor, I step through a third set of white doors in front of more white doors in front of more white doors in front of more white doors.

This time, I find myself in a small, black room inside a small, black room inside a small, black room inside a small, black room. In the dim light, I realize there are human shapes inside human shapes inside human shapes inside human shapes inside. Some are standing.

Some are crouching. Some shuffle slightly. Not one of them looks at me.

The walls are metal on top of metal on top of metal on top of metal, like those of a shipping container inside a shipping container inside a shipping container inside a shipping container, and the air is warm. I step cautiously past the shapes around shapes around shapes around shapes. My heart is still pumping with the repeated shock of entering a room inside a room inside a room inside a room. I find myself laughing again.

The house inside the house inside the house inside the house has more false corridors inside false corridors inside false corridors inside false corridors, secret rooms inside secret rooms inside secret rooms inside secret rooms, and rooms inside rooms inside rooms inside rooms where once the door behind the door behind the door behind the door closes, it will never open again unless I return from the other side.

I'm in a simple room inside a room inside a room inside a room flooded with light, with a wooden floor over a wooden floor over a wooden floor over a wooden floor. It is a copy of a copy of a copy of a copy of a room inside a room inside a room inside a room I've seen before. Any minute it could be dismantled and reinstalled somewhere else in the house inside the house inside the house inside the house. This is the wrong place for someone nearing the end of their days who wants to die after they die in a humane and harmonious environment.

I will die in one of these rooms inside rooms inside rooms inside rooms.

I question whether the house's suburban exterior around its exterior around its exterior around its exterior remains unchanged, when its interior inside its interior inside its interior inside its interior has undergone so many alterations: walls in front of walls in front of walls in front of walls in front of walls in front of walls in front of walls in front of walls in front of walls in front of walls, ceilings in front of ceilings in front of ceilings in front of ceilings under ceilings under ceilings in front of ceilings in front of ceilings in front of ceilings, rooms inside rooms inside rooms inside rooms within rooms inside rooms inside rooms inside rooms; cupboards inside cupboards inside cupboards inside cupboards morphed into doors in front of doors in front of doors and doors in front of doors in front of doors onto dead ends in front of dead ends in front of dead ends in front of dead ends; leaded floors over leaded floors over leaded floors over leaded floors and soundproof chambers inside soundproof chambers inside soundproof chambers inside soundproof chambers.

I continue through a deliberate series of bleak, small rooms inside bleak, small rooms inside bleak, small rooms inside bleak, small rooms connected by tight, mangled in-between spaces inside other in-between spaces inside other in-between spaces inside other in-between spaces. I pause in the rooms inside rooms inside rooms inside rooms that have the familiar makings of a bedroom inside a bedroom inside a bedroom inside a bedroom, a dining room inside a dining room inside a dining room inside a dining room. The in-between connective corridors inside corridors inside corridors inside corridors are confusing, a jumbled network inside a network inside a network inside a network that turns the domestic interior inside the interior inside the interior inside the interior into a treacherous maze inside a maze inside a maze inside a maze of trickery.

I still remember seeing skulls inside skulls inside skulls inside skulls inside a room inside a room inside a room inside a room inside a room inside a room, despite the fact that there were none there.

The house is reproducing existing rooms inside rooms inside rooms inside rooms in the same places inside the same places.

Through another door behind another door behind another door behind another door I arrive in the same house inside the house inside the house inside the house with its stairs over stairs over stairs over stairs, doors in front of doors in front of doors, rooms inside rooms inside rooms inside rooms; standard issue, stultifyingly familiar. The change of location is abrupt and total, from the corridors inside corridors inside corridors inside corridors into unremittingly ordinary rooms inside ordinary rooms inside ordinary rooms inside ordinary rooms. As though I had seen it all before. Behind one door behind another door behind another door behind another door a small room inside a small room inside a small room inside a small room with a mattress inside a mattress inside a mattress inside a mattress and roller blinds in front of roller blinds in front of roller blinds in front of roller blinds down, some artificial light penetrating through the slits in front of slits in front of slits in front of slits: a bedroom inside a bedroom inside a bedroom inside a bedroom; a tiny grubby room inside a tiny grubby room inside a tiny grubby room inside a tiny grubby room, a closet behind a closet behind a closet behind a closet behind a stained blanket behind a stained blanket behind a stained blanket behind a stained blanket; elsewhere the last hole inside a hole inside a hole inside a hole; a destroyed room inside a destroyed room inside a destroyed room inside a destroyed room, lined with lead sheeting on top of lead sheeting on top of lead sheeting on top of lead sheeting and fibreglass insulation over fibreglass insulation over fibreglass insulation over fibreglass insulation, studs on studs on studs on studs on the floor over the floor over the floor over the floor and on the walls in front of walls in front of walls in front of walls in preparation for more cladding over more cladding over more cladding over more cladding: the shell around the shell around the shell around the shell that is left after the removal of the totally insulated guest room inside the guest room inside the guest room inside the guest room; cellar rooms inside cellar rooms inside cellar rooms inside cellar rooms, a cellar window in front of a cellar window in front of a cellar window in front of a cellar window; some kind of a party cellar inside a party cellar inside a party cellar inside a party cellar with bare white walls in front of bare white walls in front of bare white walls in front of bare white walls, colored lights and a disco ball: a whorehouse inside a whorehouse inside a whorehouse inside a whorehouse; rooms inside rooms inside rooms inside rooms reserved for something only hinted at; a step down from a jacked-up floor over a jacked-up floor over a jacked-up floor over a jacked-up floor—under it ragged clothing, rubbish, the skin of a collapsible boat inside the skin of a collapsible boat inside the skin of a collapsible boat inside the skin of a collapsible boat, a floppy sex doll around a floppy sex doll around a floppy sex doll around a floppy sex doll, deflated—into a messy kitchen inside a messy kitchen inside a messy kitchen inside a messy kitchen with a stainless steel sink on top of a stainless steel sink on top of a stainless steel sink on top of a stainless steel sink and some crockery; hidden deeper inside the house inside the house inside the house inside the house inside the house inside the house—I have to bend down, crawl, to get through to it—a bright, clinically lit room inside a room inside a room inside a room containing a bed with white sheets on white sheets on white sheets on white sheets, a bath tub in a bath tub in a bath tub in a bath tub, a cupboard with glasses in front of a cupboard with glasses in front of a cupboard with glasses in front of a cupboard with glasses, remains of food around remains of food around remains of food around remains of food and a built-in washbasin in a washbasin in a washbasin in a washbasin: a love nest inside a love nest inside a love nest inside a love nest; an old-fashioned wooden staircase on top of a wooden staircase on top of a wooden staircase on top of a wooden staircase from the ground floor on top of the ground floor on top of the ground floor on top of the ground floor to the first floor on top of the first floor on top of the first floor on top of the first floor; a small hallway inside a hallway inside a hallway inside a hallway with twelve doors, to the stairwell inside the stairwell inside the stairwell inside the stairwell, up seven or eight steps on top of steps on top of steps on top of steps to a slightly higher coffee room inside a coffee room inside a coffee room inside a coffee room with illuminated windows in front of illuminated windows in front of illuminated windows in front of illuminated windows and curtains in front of curtains in front of curtains in front of curtains moving gently in the air, to a somewhat larger room inside a somewhat larger room inside a somewhat larger room inside a somewhat larger room which is used as a studio. It is disconcerting to find these overly familiar-seeming rooms inside rooms inside rooms inside rooms built into this pavilion inside a pavilion inside a pavilion inside a pavilion, to go through certain rooms inside rooms inside rooms inside rooms only to come unexpectedly upon more rooms inside rooms inside rooms inside rooms tucked into the body of the house inside the house inside the house inside the house, amorphous and organic in its depths and defying comprehension. These are rooms inside rooms inside rooms inside rooms that previously existed elsewhere in the house inside the house inside the house inside the house that were moved or rebuilt there.

The sequence inside the sequence inside the sequence inside the sequence of the rooms inside rooms inside rooms inside rooms is no longer the same. The top floor above the top floor above the top floor above the top floor of the house outside the house outside the house outside the house is missing, parts of rooms inside the rooms inside the rooms inside the rooms have been constructed that never existed. But it is still the house inside the house inside the house inside the house. Certain items, the socks in the corner inside the corner inside the corner inside the corner, lie in exactly the same place in one room inside a room inside a room inside a room as they do in other rooms inside rooms inside rooms inside rooms. The house inside the house inside the house inside the house is never guaranteed as authentic by a final state.

The house inside the house inside the house inside the house is a bewildering sequence inside a sequence inside a sequence inside a sequence of rooms inside rooms inside rooms inside rooms designed for all the activities of ordinary living and filled with the signs of a bachelor existence, from the inflatable dolls inside dolls inside dolls inside dolls to the electric cooking rings around electric cooking rings around electric cooking rings around electric cooking rings, from a studio inside a studio inside a studio inside a studio to a ripped out guest room inside a ripped out guest room inside a ripped out guest room inside a ripped out guest room, from the rubbish lying around to the built-in washbasin in the built-in washbasin in the built-in washbasin in the built-in washbasin —as though anyone who had once used these things that wasn't me had not been there for a long time.

A torn up floor above a floor above a floor above a floor, a completely insulated room inside a completely insulated room inside a completely insulated room inside a completely insulated room, a room inside a room inside a room inside a room in a room inside a room inside a room inside a room, a ceiling under a ceiling under a ceiling under a ceiling under a ceiling under a ceiling under a ceiling under a ceiling under a ceiling under a ceiling, a wall in front of a wall in front of a wall in front of a wall in front of a wall in front of a wall in front of a wall in front of a wall in front of a wall in front of a wall in front of a wall in front of a wall in front of a wall in front of a wall, 4 walls in front of 4 walls in front of 4 walls in front of 4 walls in front of a wall in front of a wall in front of a wall in front of a wall in front of a wall in front of a wall in front of a wall in front of a wall in front of a wall, 6 wall pieces in front of 6 wall pieces in front of 6 wall pieces in front of 6 wall pieces in front of another wall in front of another wall in front of another wall in front of another wall, a pillar around a pillar around a pillar around a pillar, a section of wall in front of a section of wall in front of a section of wall in front of a section of wall underneath the fourth ceiling underneath the ceiling underneath the ceiling underneath the ceiling, a removed and replaced section of wall in front of a removed and replaced section of wall in front of a removed and replaced section of wall in front of a removed and replaced section of wall between the walls in front of walls in front of walls in front of walls.

I imagine living entombed in the house inside the house inside the house inside the house for years in almost total isolation.

I imagine someone has come in because a door behind a door behind a door behind a door is left open. They drink a cup of coffee after a cup of coffee after a cup of coffee after a cup of coffee with me. We have a boring conversation about a boring conversation, they leave again and again and again, and don't even wonder why they were here in the first place.

I might open a wrong door behind a door behind a door behind a door at the wrong moment and plunge into an abyss inside an abyss inside an abyss inside an abyss. Whether I leave this room inside a room inside a room inside a room or stay, it is perfectly possible that I am not conscious of what is happening to me.

The non-recognizability is part of its construction strategy, which involves 'doubling' and multiplying rooms or parts of rooms inside themselves: wall in front of wall in front of wall in front of wall in front of wall in front of wall in front of wall in front of wall, ceiling below ceiling below ceiling below ceiling below ceiling below ceiling, floor on floor on floor on floor on floor on floor on floor on floor, room in room in room in room in room in room in room in room. It is a labor of representation of representation of representation of representation of representation of representation that uses the same or similar materials to replicate in the same place inside the same place inside the same place inside the same place something that already exists there, beneath one or more layers inside layers inside layers inside layers. The representation of representation of representation of representation is located exactly in front of the thing in front of the thing in front of the thing in front of the thing it is representing.

The room inside the room inside the room inside the room I'm in has one solid red plaster block around a red plaster block around a red plaster block around a red plaster block and one solid black one around another solid black one around another solid black one around another solid black one in a wall in front of a wall in front of a wall in front of a wall in front of a wall in front of an existing wall in front of a wall in front of a wall in front of a wall in front of a wall; the coffee room inside the coffee room inside the coffee room inside the coffee room, in which I spend an uneventful half-hour. It might in the meantime have completed four 360° rotations. A guest room inside a guest room inside a guest room inside a guest room has a four-metre-thick layer of insulation inside a two-metre thick layer of insulation inside a two-metre thick layer of insulation inside a two-metre thick layer of insulation. Differences, sources of possibly unexpected effects are relegated behind the walls behind the walls behind the walls behind the walls of the visible rooms inside rooms inside rooms inside rooms, and thereby put beyond the reach of normal perception.

Existing rooms inside rooms inside rooms inside rooms continue to be hidden by the same strategy of production that conceals itself in the act of the replication of replication of replication of replication.

I enter in between newly constructed sections in front of newly constructed sections in front of newly constructed sections in front of newly constructed sections and the original walls in front of walls in front of walls in front of walls, doubled windows in front of double windows in front of double windows in front of double windows in front of a solid wall in front of a solid wall in front of a solid wall in front of a solid wall, moving wall sections in front of moving wall sections in front of moving wall sections in front of moving wall sections and narrow passageways inside narrow passageways inside narrow passageways inside narrow passageways, contorted routes within routes within routes within routes between rooms inside of rooms inside of rooms inside of rooms. There is no way to distinguish between the original of the original of the original of the original and the double of the double of the double of the double, between the first structure of the structure of the structure of the structure and the new construction of the new construction of the new construction of the new construction, between the existing architecture inside the existing architecture inside the existing architecture inside the existing architecture and the added-on work in front of the added-on work in front of the added-on work in front of the added-on work. I can't distinguish any more between what has been added to the additions to the additions to the additions and what has been subtracted from the subtractions from the subtractions from the subtractions. The only way now is to again measure the hidden spaces inside the hidden spaces inside the hidden spaces inside the hidden spaces inside the hidden spaces. I can't get to the original structure outside the structure outside the structure outside the structure any more without systematically drilling apart and destroying the house inside the house inside the house inside the house.

Its source is not in the rooms inside the rooms inside the rooms inside the rooms themselves, however disquieting these may be. It lies behind what is behind them, in the area behind the area behind the area behind the area without access, or, if it were possible to reenter it, where it is impossible to tell what I am up against. The inward doubling of rooms inside rooms inside rooms inside rooms in this house inside this house inside this house inside this house, just like the construction of rooms inside rooms inside rooms inside rooms which could have been there before but were possibly not really there—this replication of the replication of the replication of the replication of what is actually or virtually there—also generates places outside of places outside of places outside of places inhabited by this unseen something inside an unseen something inside an unseen something inside an unseen something. The sinking of architectural elements inside architectural elements inside architectural elements inside architectural elements and whole rooms inside rooms inside rooms inside rooms into a second, deeper layer of space in front of a third deeper layer of space in front of a fourth deep layer of space in front of a fifth deep layer of space tips the over-familiar, the things inside things inside things inside things that are no longer perceived in their own right and which can thus stand for a home inside a home inside a home inside a home, into a negation of themselves. Anything of my own is again rendered inaccessible and unidentifiable.

It is located on the other side of familiar places inside familiar places inside familiar places inside familiar places: as the unfathomable basis of the latter it is the place inside the place inside the place inside the place inside the place where I cannot be. But it places figures inside figures inside figures inside figures in the space inside of space inside of space inside of space behind in-built rooms behind in-built rooms behind in-built rooms behind in-built rooms. Figures inside of figures inside of figures inside of figures are placed in inaccessible areas inside inaccessible areas inside inaccessible areas inside inaccessible areas, or rather, left there, like the coffin inside the coffin inside the coffin inside the coffin, the puddle around the puddle around the puddle around the puddle, the piss corner in the piss corner in the piss corner in the piss corner, the white sphere inside the white sphere inside the white sphere inside the white sphere, the black star inside the black star inside the black star inside the black star (negative cores), the pillar inside the pillar inside the pillar inside the pillar, the slime tub in the slime tub in the slime tub in the slime tub, stones in stones in stones in stones.

Whether to remain transfixed by the normality of the coffee room inside the coffee room inside the coffee room inside the coffee room, a delusion of a delusion of a delusion of a delusion of domesticity, or to sink further into the house inside the house inside the house inside the house. I am the between moving between these eight places within places within places within places.

An important wall in front of a wall in front of a wall in front of a wall in front of a wall with behind-the-wall pictures in front of behind-the-wall pictures in front of behind-the-wall pictures in front of behind-the-wall pictures of the space behind the space behind the space behind the space between the walls in front of the walls in front of the walls in front of the walls. Sometimes I get behind them myself. I make a place inside a place inside a place inside a place of my own between the in-built structures inside the in-built structures inside the in-built structures inside the in-built structures and the other, cut-off places behind the cut-off places behind the cut-off places behind the cut-off places, I move to and fro between them. I continue to document this eight-fold access in photos of photos of photos of photos and videos of videos of videos of videos of videos.

In the coffee room inside the coffee room inside the coffee room inside the coffee room with nothing happening, static; only the curtain in front of the curtain in front of the curtain in front of the curtain in front of the illuminated window in front of the illuminated window in front of the illuminated window in front of the illuminated window moving gently in the air from the ventilator in front of the ventilator in front of the ventilator in front of the ventilator in front of the ventilator positioned behind the inside wall in front of the wall in front of the wall in front of the wall. The room inside the room inside the room inside the room is something other than a normal room inside a normal room inside a normal room inside a normal room, like countless others in apartments inside apartments inside apartments inside apartments anywhere and everywhere.

I make videos of videos of videos of videos of videos of videos of dark passages inside dark passages inside dark passages inside dark passages, taken with my wildly unsteady hand-held camera and only lit with a flash-lit flashlight. In these it is possible to make out diverse, more or less legible details in front of details in front of details in front of details, some frightening items: coloured roots inside roots inside roots inside roots proliferating inwards, a human figure in front of a human figure in front of a human figure in front of a human figure, a jumbled heap of material outside a jumbled heap of material outside a jumbled heap of material outside a jumbled heap of material. I hear the sound of someone behind someone behind someone behind someone gasping and realize that it is somehow forcing its way through the internal passages inside the internal passages inside the internal passages inside the internal passages in this house inside this house inside this house inside this house, places inside places inside places inside places that I have never entered.

An interstice inside an interstice inside an interstice inside an interstice between the abyss inside the abyss inside the abyss inside the abyss and the banality of banality of banality of banality, this structure inside a structure inside a structure inside a structure leaves no room outside a room outside a room outside a room for unsuspecting innocence.

Squeezing through ever tighter spaces within spaces within spaces within spaces, feeling trapped, rubbing up against clammy walls inside clammy walls inside clammy walls inside clammy walls, I feel as if the house inside the house inside the house inside the house is actually several houses inside several houses inside several houses inside several houses. It is made from parts of parts of parts of parts of other houses inside houses inside houses inside houses but is also an autonomous thing inside a thing inside a thing inside a thing. It contains multiple houses inside multiple houses inside multiple houses inside multiple houses within itself: wall in front of wall in front of wall in front of wall in front of wall in front of wall in front of wall, wall in front of wall in front of wall in front of wall in front of wall in front of wall in front of wall in front of wall, wall behind wall behind wall behind wall behind wall behind wall behind wall behind wall, passage inside passage inside passage inside passage in room inside room inside room inside room, room inside room inside room inside room in room inside room inside room inside room.

With a change of location inside a location inside a location inside a location, the contradiction between the inconsequential ordinariness of a room inside a room inside a room inside a room and the abyss inside the abyss inside the abyss inside the abyss on the other side of another side of another side of another side is replaced by an atmosphere of penetrating, alienating alienation. The house inside the house inside the house inside the house gains additional levels on top of levels on top of levels on top of levels of legibility. The house inside the house inside the house inside the house is a number of houses inside houses inside houses inside houses, each with many rooms inside rooms inside rooms inside rooms in each room inside a room inside a room inside a room, in each room inside a room inside a room inside a room innumerable cupboards in front of cupboards in front of cupboards in front of cupboards, shelves on top of shelves on top of shelves on top of shelves, boxes in boxes in boxes in boxes, and somewhere, in each one of them inside another one inside another one inside another one, I am stood.

This is an architecture inside an architecture inside an architecture inside an architecture so turned in on itself that my journey into it leads to dead ends inside dead ends inside dead ends inside dead ends, hazards inside hazards inside hazards inside hazards: windows in front of windows in front of windows in front of windows that open only onto other windows in front of windows in front of windows in front of windows and rooms inside rooms inside rooms inside rooms bathed in light that appears natural but is actually artificial.

A whole world inside a world inside a world inside a world opens up with all sorts of things inside things inside things inside things that are not recognizable but which are there and which influence the way I feel, think, and act, how I live my daily life in here. Cladding on top of cladding on top of cladding on top of cladding in various materials alters the effect of a room inside a room inside a room inside a room without me quite being able to say why. Even the smallest protuberances and indentations on top and inside of protuberances and indentations on top and inside of protuberances and indentations on top and inside of protuberances and indentations on the finished surface in front of the finished surface in front of the finished surface in front of the finished surface of a wall in front of a wall in front of a wall in front of a wall in front of a wall arouse a response. And when that happens, the effect is registered separately from the cause of the cause of the cause of the cause. The affective state is induced, but the means by which it was created remain hidden behind the scenes—in the walls behind the walls behind the walls behind the walls and under the floors under the floors under the floors under the floors under the floors under the floors.

Even the smallest grooves inside grooves inside grooves inside grooves in a layer of plaster in front of a layer of plaster in front of a layer of plaster in front of a layer of plaster spur emotions, whereby the impact is perceived as being separate from the cause of the cause of the cause of the cause. It can happen, therefore, that I think I'm not feeling well today, although that feeling is being brought on by the room inside the room inside the room inside the room , something I cannot know. I observe this, but I never go at it directly.

There are rooms inside of rooms inside of rooms inside of rooms in this house inside this house inside this house inside this house that I can no longer access, and therefore can no longer photograph or measure. All that remains are room numbers in front of room numbers in front of room numbers in front of room numbers—and a feeling about a feeling about a feeling about a feeling—but I can't really think about the rooms inside the rooms inside the rooms inside the rooms as if they still existed normally.

I walk into intricate puzzles inside intricate puzzles inside intricate puzzles inside intricate puzzles of family dysfunction, spatial dead ends in front of spatial dead ends in front of spatial dead ends in front of spatial dead ends. A room inside a room inside a room inside a room calls to mind footage of footage of footage of footage from a police search, and raises the spectre of a world where even the most private areas of my life are increasingly vulnerable to videos of videos of videos of video surveillance. The house inside the house inside the house inside the house is an architectural cover-up, an attempt to conceal the past under a veneer of normalized normality.

What is it obscuring behind its facades in front of facades in front of facades in front of facades? The dwelling inside the dwelling inside the dwelling inside the dwelling has been stripped away. The rooms on top of rooms on top of rooms on top of rooms resemble a series of stacked blocks on top of stacked blocks on top of stacked blocks on top of stacked blocks, but close examination reveals architectural details inside architectural details inside architectural details inside architectural details, such as doorknobs inside doorknobs inside doorknobs inside doorknobs, light switches in front of light switches in front of light switches in front of light switches, and window frames in front of windows in front of windows in front of windows incised into the monotone monolith inside the monotone monolith inside the monotone monolith inside the monotone monolith that became a monument to former inhabitants; one could touch the absence of a light switch in front of a light switch in front of a light switch in front of a light switch, fingers meeting the ghosts of the future.

Two luminous windows in front of two luminous windows in front of two luminous windows in front of two luminous windows in a room inside a room inside a room inside a room bestow a confrontational aliveness. I sometimes feel the windows in front of windows in front of windows in front of windows in this house inside this house inside this house inside this house are looking at me.

I feel that the world behind the world behind the world behind the world has suddenly been sucked into a void inside a void inside a void inside a void at my back with the closing of a door behind a door behind a door behind a door. The sense that spaces inside spaces inside spaces inside spaces are smaller than they should be, and blocked windows in front of blocked windows in front of blocked windows in front of blocked windows at several points in the house inside the house inside the house inside the house to disconnect a visitor from the exterior of the exterior of the exterior of the exterior.

There are exposed windows in front of windows in front of windows in front of windows in the kitchens inside the kitchens inside the kitchens. After leaving I pass through a sitting room inside a sitting room inside a sitting room inside a sitting room with lace doilies and shopping items that needed to be put away, and continue upstairs above the upstairs above the upstairs above the upstairs to yet more claustrophobic windowless rooms inside claustrophobic windowless rooms inside claustrophobic windowless rooms inside claustrophobic windowless rooms.

I excavate further down through the layers of paper on top of paper on top of paper on top of paper, to uncover a bedroom inside a bedroom inside a bedroom inside a bedroom with white walls in front of white walls in front of white walls in front of white walls, a white wardrobe in front of a white wardrobe in front of a white wardrobe in front of a white wardrobe , white bedding on white bedding on white bedding on white bedding, and a thick white carpet on thick white carpet on thick white carpet on thick white carpet. Another body inside a body inside a body inside a body is propped up in the corner in a black garbage bag inside a black garbage bag inside a black garbage bag inside a black garbage bag. I have been caught in a loop within a loop within a loop within a loop.

An attic inside an attic inside an attic inside an attic, above a bedroom inside a bedroom inside a bedroom inside a bedroom, is loaded with symbols of domestic space over symbols of domestic space over symbols of domestic space over symbols of domestic space. But the garret inside the garret inside the garret inside the garret represents another dead end in front of a dead end in front of a dead end in front of a dead end.

A baby gate in front of a baby gate in front of a baby gate in front of a baby gate in front of the door in front of the door in front of the door in front of the door provokes more questions. The questions are impossible to answer; the door behind the door behind the door behind the door is locked. The attic door behind the attic door behind the attic door behind the attic door is followed by a vertiginous view back down a tight helical staircase inside a tight helical staircase inside a tight helical staircase inside a tight helical staircase.

I run down multiple flights of stairs on top of multiple flights of stairs on top of multiple flights of stairs on top of multiple flights of stairs into a basement inside a basement inside a basement inside a basement, the subterranean area where the most horrific secrets are hidden and hidden again and hidden again and hidden again. I encounter a small room inside a room inside a room inside a room with floral wallpaper on top of floral wallpaper on top of floral wallpaper on top of floral wallpaper, and then a doorway behind a doorway behind a doorway behind a doorway to a bleak room inside a bleak room inside a bleak room inside a bleak room with twine twisted and hanging on the wall in front of the wall in front of the wall in front of the wall and an overturned chair inside an overturned chair inside an overturned chair inside an overturned chair. Is it the site of a suicide on top of the site of a suicide on top of the site of a suicide on top of the site of a suicide or perhaps a hanging in front of a hanging in front of a hanging in front of a hanging? Outside this dark, insulated space outside another dark, insulated space outside another dark, insulated space outside another dark, insulated space is a stack of paper towels and cupcakes, like one would find at a child's birthday party. The gaiety, which marks the celebration of a birth, is overshadowed by the distinct feeling the room inside the room inside the room inside the room could function as a torture chamber around a torture chamber around a torture chamber around a torture chamber.

There is another secret passage inside a secret passage inside a secret passage inside a secret passage behind a bookshelf behind a bookshelf behind a bookshelf behind a bookshelf that has been pulled away from a wall in front of a wall in front of a wall in front of a wall in front of a wall, a low-ceilinged hallway inside a low-ceilinged hallway inside a low-ceilinged hallway inside a low-ceilinged hallway brings me to the end of a passageway inside a passageway inside a passageway inside a passageway blocked off by a storeroom door in front of a storeroom door in front of a storeroom door in front of a storeroom door, which is chained and padlocked in place. If the storeroom inside the storeroom inside the storeroom inside the storeroom was open, a tiny chamber inside a chamber inside a chamber inside a chamber at the end of the corridor inside the corridor inside the corridor inside the corridor would contain a stained crib mattress on top of a stained crib mattress on top of a stained crib mattress on top of a stained crib mattress. The sound of a crying baby; innocence suffocated by the depths of this monstrous house inside a house inside a house inside a house.

I stare at damage to the walls inside walls inside walls inside walls and the floorboards on top of floorboards on top of floorboards on top of floorboards. What is that shape inside the shape inside the shape inside the shape on the wall in front of the wall in front of the wall in front of the wall? A horse head inside a horse head inside a horse head inside a horse head? Australia inside Australia inside Australia inside Australia? The images become mnemonics for knowledge that ultimately resides outside the house outside the house outside the house inside the house inside the house inside the house.

Distorted doublings reveal that which has been hidden behind the hidden behind the hidden behind the hidden, and these disturbances to the expected order provoke a re-consideration of the house inside the house inside the house inside the house, the home inside the home inside the home inside the home, and the domestic realm inside the domestic realm inside the domestic realm inside the domestic realm.

More creepy basements inside basements inside basements inside basements with one bare bulb and unexplainable holes inside of holes inside of holes inside of holes dug in the middle of the floor on top of the floor on top of the floor on top of the floor; basements inside basements inside basements inside basements like this all over, locked up and untouched since the '40s, ignored but not forgotten by the figments of people going about their lives in the rooms inside rooms inside rooms inside rooms above.

I confront the lies I tell myself to keep living after traumas of unspeakable proportions: the untruths of modern life, spatial and perceptual manipulation through various media—mirrors inside mirrors inside mirrors inside mirrors, photographs inside photographs inside photographs inside photographs, surveillance video inside surveillance video inside surveillance video inside surveillance video.

I don't know where I can go from here. I could go on running on the spot, just go until the house inside the house inside the house inside the house pushes me out or swallows me even deeper. I could systematically dismantle the house inside the house inside the house inside the house.

It's just chance that out of necessity I'm here. I'd love to get out.

By now the house inside the house inside the house inside the house has become independent. It has its own inner dynamics. The sheer amount means that I can't distinguish any more between what has been added to the additions to the additions to the additions and what has been subtracted from the subtractions from the subtractions from the subtractions. There is no way now of fully documenting the documenting of the documenting of the documenting of what has happened in the house inside the house inside the house inside the house. The only way now would be to measure the hidden spaces inside the hidden spaces inside the hidden spaces inside the hidden spaces inside the hidden spaces. No-one could get to the original structure outside the structure outside the structure outside the structure any more without systematically drilling apart and destroying the house inside the house inside the house inside the house. The layers of lead inside the layers of lead inside the layers of lead inside the layers of lead mean you can't even X-ray it.

Because I spend all my time here, I have to accept the rooms inside rooms inside rooms inside rooms as they are, and accept the most recently built as perfectly normal. And even though the light in this room inside a room inside a room inside a room is from a lamp behind a lamp behind a lamp and the air is produced by a ventilator behind a ventilator behind a ventilator behind a ventilator, by now the atmosphere seems quite normal to me. I need normal light in front of light in front of light in front of light and recirculated air here.

This is the work of something insulating itself.

There are rooms inside rooms inside rooms inside rooms completely insulated with lead on top of lead on top of lead on top of lead, glass fibre on glass fibre on glass fibre on glass fibre, sound-proofing materials on sound-proofing materials on sound-proofing materials on sound-proofing materials and other stuff. I am right in the middle of it and surrender to the house inside the house inside the house inside the house. Whether I am insulating myself from the world, or whether it's a breakthrough—I don't really know.

All this takes a long time. I wouldn't like it if the only thing about the house inside the house inside the house inside the house is that I live in it. Because that would mean it was just my cell inside my cell inside my cell inside my cell. Whether it's a place of refuge. I don't know. Anyway, now I've got a guest room inside a guest room inside a guest room inside a guest room. Maybe some others might like to fester away here instead of me.

A wall in front of a wall in front of a wall in front of a wall in front of a wall in front of a wall in front of a wall in front of a wall in front of a wall in front of a wall in front of a wall in front of a wall in front of a wall in front of a wall, a wall behind a wall behind a wall behind a wall behind a wall behind a wall behind a wall behind a wall behind a wall behind a wall, a passage inside a passage inside a passage inside a passage inside a passage in room inside a room inside a room inside a room inside a room, a room inside a room inside a room inside a room in a room inside a room inside a room inside a room, a passage inside a passage inside a passage inside a passage in a room inside a room inside a room inside a room, a wall in front of a wall in front of a wall in front of a wall in front of a wall in front of a wall in front of a wall in front of a wall in front of a wall in front of a wall in front of a wall in front of a wall in front of a wall in front of a wall, a room inside a room inside a room inside a room in a room inside a room inside a room inside a room, a room inside a room inside a room inside a room in a room inside a room inside a room inside a room, a room inside a room inside a room inside a room in a room inside a room inside a room inside a room, a red stone inside a red stone inside a red stone inside a red stone behind a room inside a room inside a room inside a room, lead on top of lead on top of lead on top of lead around a room inside a room inside a room inside a room, lead on top of lead on top of lead on top of lead in a floor beneath a floor beneath a floor beneath a floor, light around a room inside a room inside a room inside a room, light around a room inside a room inside a room inside a room, a wall in front of a wall in front of a wall in front of a wall in front of a wall in front of a wall in front of a wall in front of a wall in front of a wall in front of a wall in front of a wall in front of a wall in front of a wall, a figure inside a figure inside a figure inside a figure in a wall in front of a wall in front of a wall in front of a wall in front of a wall, a wall in front of a wall in front of a wall in front

of a wall in front of a wall in front of a wall in front of
a wall in front of a wall in front of a wall in front of a
wall in front of a wall in front of a wall in front of a wall
in front of a wall, a wall in front of a wall in front of a
wall in front of a wall in front of a wall in front of a wall
in front of a wall in front of a wall in front of a wall in
front of a wall in front of a wall in front of a wall in front
of a wall in front of a wall, a room inside a room inside
a room inside a room in a room inside a room inside a
room inside a room, a wall in front of a wall in front of
a wall in front of a wall in front of a wall in front of a
wall in front of a wall in front of a wall in front of a wall
in front of a wall in front of a wall in front of a wall in
front of a wall in front of a wall, a wall in front of a wall
in front of a wall in front of a wall in front of a wall in
front of a wall in front of a wall in front of a wall in front
of a wall in front of a wall in front of a wall in front of a
wall in front of a wall in front of a wall, a wall in front
of a wall in front of a wall in front of a wall in front of a
wall in front of a wall in front of a wall in front of a wall
in front of a wall in front of a wall in front of a wall in
front of a wall in front of a wall in front of a wall, a ceiling under a ceiling under a ceiling under a ceiling under
a ceiling under a ceiling under a ceiling under a ceiling
under a ceiling under a ceiling, a section of wall in front
of a section of wall in front of a section of wall in front
of a section of wall in front of a wall in front of a wall in

front of a wall in front of a wall in front of a wall in front of a wall in front of a wall in front of a wall in front of a wall, a wall in front of a wall in front of a wall in front of a wall in front of a wall in front of a wall in front of a wall in front of a wall in front of a wall in front of a wall in front of a wall in front of a wall in front of a wall in front of a wall in front of a wall, a section of wall in front of a section of wall in front of a section of wall in front of a section of wall in front of a wall in front of a wall in front of a wall in front of a wall in front of a wall in front of a wall in front of a wall in front of a wall in front of a wall in front of a wall, a wall in front of a wall in front of a wall in front of a wall in front of a wall in front of a wall in front of a wall in front of a wall in front of a wall in front of a wall...

I start to build complete rooms inside rooms inside rooms inside rooms with floors on top of floors on top of floors on top of floors, walls in front of walls in front of walls in front of walls and ceilings below ceilings below ceilings below ceilings, that you can't see as a room inside a room inside a room inside a room in a room inside a room inside a room inside a room or a room around a room around a room around a room around a room around a room around a room around a room. There is a constant stream of new rooms inside rooms inside rooms inside rooms made from various materials around various materials around various materials around various materials. Some of them—imperceptibly—rise up, sink back down or complete a full rotation. The house inside the house inside the house inside the house is really about the fact that I am always starting again.

The first time I built a room inside a room inside a room inside a room, I had no idea that's what I had done. It was something else that told me.

I don't notice that the room inside the room inside the room inside the room has rotated once right round. Of course I can't know what will happen. I might open the wrong door behind the wrong door behind the wrong door behind the wrong door at the wrong moment and plunge into an abyss inside an abyss inside an abyss inside an abyss.

There are rooms inside rooms inside rooms inside rooms which are not recognisable as such, but which have an effect, change my mood or my way of behaving.

As soon as I have built a stone inside a stone inside a stone inside a stone into a wall in front of a wall in front of a wall in front of a wall in front of a wall—a red one or a totally black one—after a while I don't know where it is any more, and the same thing happens again and again and again and again and again and again. It's like that with a wall in front of a wall in front of a wall in front of a wall in front of a wall and exactly the same with a room inside a room inside a room inside a room. As soon as I spend any time in a room inside a room inside a room inside a room, I accept it as a normal room inside a room inside a room inside a room.

A whole world within a world within a world within a world opens up with all sort of things that are not recognisable but which are there and which influence the way I feel, think and act, how I live my daily life. The fact that the room inside a room inside a room inside a room is rotating without my knowing it can alter the direction I walk in. Cladding on top of cladding on top of cladding on top of cladding in various materials around materials around materials around materials can alter the effect of a room inside a room inside a room inside a room without me quite being able to say why. Even the smallest protuberances on protuberances on protuberances on protuberances and indentations in indentations in indentations in indentations on the finished surface in front of the surface in front of the surface in front of the surface of a wall in front of a wall in front of a wall in front of a wall in front of a wall can arouse a response in me. And when that happens, the effect is registered separately from the cause of the cause of the cause of the cause. So sometimes I might say, I'm having a bad day today: the feeling has been induced by the room inside a room inside a room inside a room but I can't know that. I observe these things. But I don't set out to make them happen.

I spend more and more months digging up the whole house inside the house inside the house inside the house. I manage to reconstruct one room inside a room inside a room inside a room more or less as it was. 7 by 2.76 by 0.25 metres. It has five individual windows in front of windows in front of windows in front of windows. The ceiling below the ceiling below the ceiling below the ceiling goes up and down continuously, imperceptibly. The room inside the room inside the room inside the room remains in place for a whole year. It is brutal work, and when I think about it, it all scarcely seems credible. I try to become even more concentrated, construct poised rooms inside rooms inside rooms inside rooms, well-balanced. Whatever I take away on one side is put back on the other. Amongst other things I make a pillar inside a pillar inside a pillar inside a pillar, try to get to the point in the house inside the house inside the house inside the house. Build a room inside a room inside a room inside a room somewhere else almost exactly like the existing room inside a room inside a room inside a room here. Go specially all that way and then put it up in ten days.

Do you know the way people on spaceships beam themselves from one place to another? When I am back here again I try to imagine the things that are happening there. I could imagine repeatedly building a more or less identical room inside a room inside a room inside a room from memory in various different places inside places inside places inside places, to get back here again maybe. But I don't really know. They look unremarkable and meaningless, but at the same time they freeze everything.

I'm in a big room inside a bigger room inside a bigger room inside a bigger room, looking out of a window in front of a window in front of a window in front of a window. In front of it: a substituted piece of wall in front of a substituted piece of wall in front of a substituted piece of wall in front of a substituted piece of wall.

The motivation is there's nothing else to do. I keep having to test the thing inside the thing inside the thing inside the thing I have committed myself to, keep having to ask myself the question inside the question inside the question inside the question, whether it's at all worth doing.

I tried at one stage not to leave one part of the house inside the house inside the house inside the house for an indefinite period. In my search for immediacy I became immediate. When that happens I can't talk. But I also seek out other moments, where I stand next to the self beside myself beside myself beside myself.

I am seeking to get closer to things inside things inside things inside things.

There are different layers on top of layers on top of layers on top of layers that merge into one another—that I can't control.

I was once registered as having a perceptual disorder and as being mentally ill, but I had only told them what I was doing at the time. I didn't lie. I will build more rooms inside more rooms inside more rooms inside more rooms, a room inside a room inside a room inside a room that I don't perceive as a room inside a room inside a room inside a room in a room inside a room inside a room inside a room or a room inside a room inside a room inside a room round a room round a room round a room round a room, then suddenly a wall in front of a wall in front of a wall in front of a wall in front of a wall is there and then gone again. I look at a wall in front of a wall in front of a wall in front of a wall in front of a wall and am interested in any unevennesses on its surface in front of its surface in front of its surface in front of its surface: the tiniest hole in the tiniest hole in the tiniest hole in the tiniest hole, the slightest protuberance on the slightest protuberance on the slightest protuberance on the slightest protuberance.

It even seems illogical to me to build these rooms inside rooms inside rooms inside rooms at all. I have the feeling that I needn't build them at all.

My experiments involve going into a room inside a room inside a room inside a room, leaving it again, hoping that the experience will linger there. Perhaps all these rooms inside rooms inside rooms inside rooms are also a preparation for my one day not having to enter any more rooms inside rooms inside rooms inside rooms.

I am interested in distortions. I sit looking at them for hours, for days on end. And then there are screams screamed over screams over screams over screams, they are always there. Repeated screams over screams over screams over screams. I see the human scream screamed over screams over screams over screams. I dig holes inside holes inside holes inside holes, bury myself. I hope the screams screamed over screams over screams over screams will stay behind in the room inside the room inside the room inside the room after I leave it. Here another female art student has been killed.

I crawl inside totally insulated boxes inside totally insulated boxes inside totally insulated boxes inside totally insulated boxes. If I am sitting in a box inside a box inside a box inside a box I can't hear the screaming screamed over screams over screams over screams outside any more... I hope that life will be the difference between a full and an empty box inside a box inside a box inside a box. I introduce a layer of insulation on top of a layer of insulation on top of a layer of insulation on top of a layer of insulation into a room inside a room inside a room inside a room. I use my technical skills to completely insulate the room inside the room inside the room inside the room as far as the senses are concerned. I come into an unremarkable passage inside a passage inside a passage inside a passage, then behind a veneered, everyday door in front of a veneered, everyday door in front of a veneered, everyday door in front of a veneered, everyday door, reinforced with steel beams inside steel beams inside steel beams inside steel beams, I am confronted with a cross-section of the insulating materials on top of insulating materials on top of insulating materials on top of insulating materials. I feel strong pressure on my ears if I bend down into the black, unfathomable depth inside holes inside holes insidbelow the black, unfathomable depth below the black, unfathomable depth below the black, unfathomable depthe holes. If I had gone into the room inside the room inside the room inside the room the door behind the door behind the door behind the door would have swung shut. There is no way of opening it either from inside or from outside. I am gone. Whether it is a hole inside a hole inside a hole inside a hole or a window in front of a window in front of a window in front of a window, I don't know, I never went in.

A child falls into a deep freeze inside a deep freeze inside a deep freeze inside a deep freeze, while a woman is standing right next to it doing the washing-up.

I take photos of photos of photos of photos of the place inside the place inside the place inside the place inside the place where the students were murdered. Later there are flowers laying on flowers laying on flowers laying on flowers there. I keep coming back. And then I come to the conclusion that places inside places inside places inside places just look the same although quite different things have happened there.

One of the doors behind a door behind a door behind a door has gone again. One of the doors behind a door behind a door behind a door behind a door leads to a light, a relatively large room inside a room inside a room inside a room that has openings behind openings behind openings behind openings to the outside. Up to fourteen windows in front of windows in front of windows in front of windows one in front of the other in order to change the way the light falls. That's why the walls in front of the walls in front of the walls in front of the walls are so thick.

There are several layers of paint on top of paint on top of the paint on top of paint on the glass in front of the glass in front of the glass in front of the glass. No light gets through. But it creates the impression of a window in front of a window in front of a window in front of a window. I push this section of wall in front of a section of wall in front of a section of wall in front of a section of wall in front of it, in front of the opening out to the back.

I am standing in front of an important wall in front of a wall in front of a wall in front of a wall in front of a wall, where I lean the behind-the-wall pictures of the behind-the-wall pictures of the behind-the-wall pictures of the behind-the-wall pictures or the behind-the-wall stones inside the behind-the-wall-stones inside the behind-the-wall-stones inside the behind-the-wall-stones or sometimes I get behind it myself. At the moment it is empty.

Of course there are original walls behind the walls behind the walls behind the walls, otherwise the house outside the house outside the house outside the house wouldn't stand up. The colour on top of the colour on top of the colour on top of the colour is not just on the surface of the surface of the surface of the surface.

There are leftovers of leftovers of leftovers of leftovers from buckets of mortar in buckets of mortar in buckets of mortar in buckets of mortar, or not, some are plaster. Left-over mortar in a bucket inside leftover mortar in a bucket inside leftover mortar in a bucket inside leftover mortar in a bucket. I take it in my hand and make it into a ball around a ball around a ball around a ball. I end up with twenty or thirty. I stick these all together and that makes one big ball around another big ball around another big ball around another big ball. It gives me new material to close up a small wall in front of a wall in front of a wall in front of a wall in front of a wall or some opening in an opening in an opening in an opening. The other stuff is newspaper, soaked and compressed. Amazingly enough it's super tough, a great material, a great building material, utterly simple material. You can apply thin layers of plaster on top of plaster on top of plaster on top of plaster only consisting of a surface on a surface on a surface on a surface. Big boards in front of big boards in front of big boards in front of big boards in front that are made from a lot of smaller parts around a lot of other smaller parts around a lot of other smaller parts around a lot of other smaller parts, starting again and again and again and again and again and again in different places. The amazing thing is that it's simply a matter of doing.

I can stand in front of a wall in front of a wall in front of a wall in front of a wall in front of a wall in front of a wall in front of a wall in front of a wall in front of a wall for hours on end, looking at it. I can do that once, twice, for a whole month or even longer, and then at some point I can tell everyone about that wall.

All this from the sheer boredom of boredom. All jobs involve repeated actions.

The other door behind the door behind the door behind the door of the sorting-room inside the sorting-room inside the sorting-room inside the sorting-room leads into a little room inside a little room inside a little room inside a little room with a coffee table and also the central switching station inside the central switching station inside the central switching station inside the central switching station, the fuse box inside the fuse box inside the fuse box inside the fuse box. It's a room inside a room inside a room inside a room that can rotate on its own axis. A window in front of a window in front of a window in front of a window is lit from behind. It has a pleasant, friendly atmosphere, but which is obviously wholly artificial. There is a warm halogen lamp in front of a warm halogen lamp in front of a warm halogen lamp in front of a warm halogen lamp.

I have the feeling again that my brain has stopped and my body is going on turning, tighter and tighter until it tears. The ventilator in front of the ventilator in front of the ventilator in front of the ventilator in front of the ventilator is not on at the moment. I like it when there's a gentle flow of air. At the moment I feel more as though the window in front of the window in front of the window in front of the window is looking at me. Like the two bright windows behind the windows behind the windows behind the windows outside. The thing is that I am always waiting to see what will happen. I can never know in advance. Sometimes I have the feeling that people suddenly just appear. And then there might be a kind of vortex inside a vortex inside a vortex inside a vortex, a loud droning noise.

I take yet another door behind a door behind a door behind a door off its hinges, the one at the very back. Now I can get behind the rotating room inside the room inside the room inside the room. It's very difficult to take photographs of photographs of photographs of photographs of the rooms inside the rooms inside the rooms inside the rooms . You partly have to cut the rooms inside the rooms inside the rooms inside the rooms open again.

There are more things stored here. These are quite lightly built walls in front of walls in front of walls in front of walls that I have already bricked some things into. I always have to be sure that I am not overdoing it.

When I open it I get to a wall in front of a wall in front of a wall in front of a wall in front of a wall in front of a wall that sounds less and less solid.

Some bits are more rickety, some bits are more solid. You can't tell just by tapping. The smaller the room inside the room inside the room inside the room , the lighter it is. I can't get any more big, heavy parts into it.

Downstairs a hall inside a hall inside a hall inside a hall goes to a door behind a door behind a door behind a door at the back that leads into a guest room inside a guest room inside a guest room inside a guest room, the heavily insulated room inside the heavily insulated room inside the heavily insulated room inside the heavily insulated room. Inside it there is a grille in front of a grille in front of a grille in front of a grille in the wall in front of the wall in front of the wall in front of the wall that I could leave by, through more passages inside passages inside passages inside passages at the back. I could basically turn the house inside the house inside the house inside the house inside-out from here. I could get out through shafts inside shafts inside shafts inside shafts and empty spaces. This is my escape route.

Another double door in front of another double door in front of another double door in front of another double door in the hall inside the hall inside the hall inside the hall, just left of the main door behind the main door behind the main door behind the main door, leads into a narrow, completely dark room inside a room inside a room inside a room. Opposite the door behind the door behind the door behind the door there is a wall of sound-absorbing material in front of sound-absorbing material in front of sound-absorbing material in front of sound-absorbing material. Is there another room inside a room inside a room inside a room behind that? It's the shape of a house in the house in the house in the house hanging upside down. I put more layers on top of layers on top of layers on top of layers in front of it. The shape of the house inside the house inside the house inside the house is hanging here like an elephant, super-heavy. The wall in front of the wall in front of the wall in front of the wall is jacked up again and various layers on top of layers on top of layers on top of layers have been put in front of it. Behind it, separated off, is the narrow room inside a room inside a room inside a room with windows behind windows behind windows behind windows facing what I think I remember is the street in front of the street in front of the street in front of the street.

Now I am going up another three steps on top of steps on top of steps on top of steps into a little room inside a little room inside a little room inside a little room. This room inside a room inside a room inside a room that has been reproduced a lot of times. An external roller blind over an external roller blind over an external roller blind over an external roller blind is down outside the window behind the window behind the window behind the window. Under the floor below the floor below the floor below the floor is a bird cage around a bird cage around a bird cage around a bird cage, inflatable dolls inside inflatable dolls inside inflatable dolls inside inflatable dolls. There's another door behind a door behind a door behind a door, and when I open it I see yet another door behind the door behind the door behind the door behind it, but instead of the door behind the door behind the door behind the door opening, the whole wall in front of the wall in front of the wall in front of the wall moves away. This leads further into the house inside the house inside the house inside the house: a little kitchen inside a kitchen inside a kitchen inside a kitchen with a stainless steel sink. There is a shaft going upwards that links the different floors between floors between floors between floors. The kitchen inside the kitchen inside the kitchen inside the kitchen is a room inside a room inside a room inside a room without a window in front of a window in front of a window in front of a window. Cables inside cables inside cables inside cables, light switches on top of light switches on top of light switches on top of light switches, a cup in a cup in a cup in a cup, denser materials. After the kitchen inside the kitchen inside the kitchen inside the kitchen I open another door behind a door behind a door behind a door into a little room inside a room inside a room inside a room made of cement bricks in front of cement bricks in front of cement bricks in front of cement bricks, a room inside a room inside a room inside a room like a storeroom inside a storeroom inside a storeroom inside a storeroom. But why does the door behind the door behind the door behind the door open inwards into this room inside a room inside a room inside a room? It means you can't use it. There is another wall in front of wall that can be opened, and I squeeze through a passage inside a passage inside a passage inside a passage. It gets narrower and damper too. There is wonderfully colourful mould here. And then I go into a room inside a room inside a room inside a room of private things: dead animals inside dead animals inside dead animals inside dead animals, heads inside heads inside heads inside heads, a hand in a hand in a hand in a hand, a stomach in a stomach in a stomach in a stomach, a heavy white ball inside a heavy white ball inside a heavy white ball inside a heavy white ball, a black star in a black star in a black star in a black star, covered in four layers of sound-absorbing material.

What is behind the last window behind the last window behind the last window behind the last window behind the last window behind the last window? Behind the last window behind the last window behind the last window behind the last window behind the last window behind the last window that you can open there is another window behind the window behind the window behind the window. You can get up on to the window sill on top of the window sill on top of the window sill on top of the window sill and see old photos of photos of photos of photos in the gap inside the gaps inside the gaps inside the gaps between. I have left pictures of pictures of pictures of pictures and pieces of furniture on top of pieces of furniture on top of pieces of furniture on top of pieces of furniture where they were and built a new room inside a room inside a room inside a room. In the gap inside the gap inside the gap inside the gap I hang from a hook from a hook from a hook from a hook. Presumably I can still pupate here.

I dream about taking the whole house inside a house inside a house inside a house away with me and building it somewhere else. Somewhere in a corner inside a corner inside a corner inside a corner there must be a large lady around a lady around a lady around a lady who constantly makes children inside children inside children inside children. What is behind the last window behind the last window behind the last window behind the last window behind the last window behind the last window? I raise it and stare at a solid white wall in front of a solid white wall in front of a solid white wall in front of a solid white wall.

And the corpses on top of corpses on top of corpses on top of corpses are lying in a cellar inside a cellar inside a cellar inside a cellar. Corpses on top of corpses on top of corpses on top of corpses always lie in a cellar inside a cellar inside a cellar inside a cellar. Perhaps I am the one that can't get out.

The table over the table over the table over the table is laid, decorated with a small cherry blossom twig. And then more rooms inside of rooms inside of rooms inside of rooms that I have already been into. Through the rooms inside of rooms inside of rooms inside of rooms, the different floors on top of floors on top of floors on top of floors, up a ladder in front of a ladder in front of a ladder in front of a ladder, on all fours, through gaps inside gaps inside gaps inside gaps, past moveable walls in front of walls in front of walls in front of walls. Windows in front of windows in front of windows in front of windows, the few that there are, can be opened, looking out onto other windows in front of windows in front of windows in front of windows and ultimately a solid wall in front of a solid wall in front of a solid wall in front of a solid wall. The light is artificial. I become disorientated again. There is a strong sense of being somehow insulated. The silence makes itself felt.

A narrow passage inside a narrow passage inside a narrow passage inside a narrow passage with a short flight of steps over steps over steps over steps and two doors in front of two doors in front of two doors in front of two doors, a bedroom inside a bedroom inside a bedroom inside a bedroom, a kitchen area inside a kitchen area inside a kitchen area inside a kitchen area. Transplanted rooms inside transplanted rooms inside transplanted rooms inside transplanted rooms. A different configuration of rooms inside rooms inside rooms inside rooms.

A plaster mask in front of a plaster mask in front of a plaster mask in front of a plaster mask has been leant in a corner inside a corner inside a corner inside a corner of a bedroom inside a bedroom inside a bedroom inside a bedroom. An impression of a face in front of a face in front of a face in front of a face.

Someone has left tracks inside tracks inside tracks inside tracks. Wear and tear in the rooms inside rooms inside rooms inside rooms: stains on stains on stains on stains on the carpet over the carpet over the carpet over the carpet, items of clothing, clutter, a canoe inside a canoe inside a canoe inside a canoe underneath the bedroom inside the bedroom inside the bedroom inside the bedroom on stilts on stilts on stilts on stilts, photographs of photographs of photographs of photographs in the kitchen inside the kitchen inside the kitchen—stuck to the fridge door in front of the fridge door in front of the fridge door in front of the fridge door or pinned to the doorframe inside the doorframe inside the doorframe inside the doorframe.

I build more rooms inside rooms inside rooms inside rooms.

This crate inside a crate inside a crate inside a crate inside a crate contains a body around a body around a body around a body not to be found in another crate inside a crate inside a crate inside a crate inside a crate. Beyond this wall in front of a wall in front of a wall in front of a wall in front of a wall there is a room inside a room inside a room inside a room which might still not be there at all. Outside this window behind a window behind a window behind a window is another window behind a window behind a window behind a window through which daylight gleams, or maybe there is not. Awareness still that something was murdered in this room inside a room inside a room inside a room.

Padded with glass wool on top of glass wool on top of glass wool on top of glass wool, lined with Styrofoam on top of Styrofoam on top of Styrofoam on top of Styrofoam, plaster on plaster on plaster on plaster and lead on lead on lead on lead, the room inside the room inside the room inside the room is silent, and yet surrounded by the same polyphonic hum.

What is within the house within the house within the house within the house must stay here. An intercalary mass.

Strange leftovers moving over strange leftovers over strange leftovers over strange leftovers appear in the beam of my torch.

Unused materials have been stored in these in between spaces in between spaces in between spaces in between spaces, but they are also filled with figures inside figures inside figures inside figures and spaces behind spaces behind spaces behind spaces that have no space elsewhere because no space behind a space behind a space behind a space was given to them, or because they were undesirable.

When converted rooms inside rooms inside rooms inside rooms are re-installed or copied in other spaces behind spaces behind spaces behind spaces the construction of a space behind a space behind a space behind a space behind them, inaccessible and unused, a remnant, is foregrounded. The place behind the place behind the place behind the place where I am not and don't belong imposes itself.

I record various videos of videos of videos of videos of videos documenting the penetration of such dark, overgrown and claustrophobic zones within zones within zones within zones.

In the hindmost layers on top of layers on top of layers on top of layers of the house inside the house inside the house inside the house is an inflatable sex doll inside an inflatable sex doll inside an inflatable sex doll inside an inflatable sex doll amongst all kinds of garbage in the space of a false floor on top of a false floor on top of a false floor on top of a false floor. Far below a cellar inside cellar inside a cellar inside a cellar: a brothel/disco. Recently I have broken vertically through the layers inside layers inside layers inside layers of the house inside the house inside the house inside the house.

I am embroiled beyond my understanding. The over-exertion is a strategy inside a strategy inside a strategy inside a strategy. Pushing my way through manholes inside manholes inside manholes inside manholes and corridors inside corridors inside corridors inside corridors, and reaching the red-light area of a previously unknown room inside a previously unknown room inside a previously unknown room inside a previously unknown room, I am left with the suspicion that I might have gone a different way, and what would have happened then? I might open a wrong door in front of a wrong door in front of a wrong door in front of a wrong door at the wrong time and get lost for good.

The gaps inside gaps inside gaps inside gaps make it possible to build the rooms inside rooms inside rooms inside rooms that were previously missing, rooms inside rooms inside rooms inside rooms for making out with women on top of women on top of women on top of women and sleeping with them, abject zones inside abject zones inside abject zones inside abject zones. The closer I move towards it, the further away it gets.

I return to document the rooms I entered earlier. I mark the doors again with numbers:

1. wall in front of a wall in front of a wall in front of a wall in front of a wall in front of a wall in front of a wall in front of a wall in front of a wall in front of a wall in front of a wall in front of a wall in front of a wall in front of a wall in front of a wall, chalky sandstone and mortar, white 118 x 236 cm, W 48 cm / 2. wall behind a wall behind a wall behind a wall behind a wall behind a wall behind a wall behind a wall behind a wall behind a wall, chipboard on chipboard on chipboard on chipboard on wood, white 128 x 136 cm. W 8 cm / 3. corridor inside a corridor inside a corridor inside a corridor inside a corridor in a room inside a room inside a room inside a room, wood and chipboards on wood and chipboards on wood and chipboards on wood and chipboards, grey wooden stairs on grey wooden stairs on grey wooden stairs on grey wooden stairs, white walls in front of walls in front of walls in front of walls and ceiling below ceiling below ceiling below ceiling 59 x 62 x 97 cm, W 6-40 cm / 4. room inside a room inside a room inside a room within a room inside a room inside a room inside a room, chipboards on chipboards

on chipboards on chipboards on a construction made of steel on steel on steel on steel and wood along with posts, 2 doors, 1 window, 1 lamp, 1 radiator, grey carpet on grey carpet on grey carpet on grey carpet, white walls in front of walls in front of walls in front of walls and ceiling below ceiling below ceiling below ceiling, detached, ca. 120-200 cm distance from the outer room inside a room inside a room inside a room 98 x 156 x 71 cm. W 6-48 cm / 5. red stone inside red stone inside red stone inside red stone behind a room inside a room inside a room inside a room 18 x 5 cm / 6. lead around a room inside a room inside a room inside a room 79 x 196 x 92 cm, W 0.8 cm / 7. bedroom inside a bedroom inside a bedroom inside a bedroom, lead in the ground 208 x 306 cm, W 0.8 cm / 8. corridor inside a corridor inside a corridor inside a corridor in a room inside a room inside a room inside a room, wood and chipboards on wood and chipboards on wood and chipboards on wood and chipboards, grey wooden stairs on grey wooden stairs on grey wooden stairs on grey wooden stairs, white walls in front of white walls in front of white walls in front of white walls and ceiling below ceiling below ceiling below ceiling 47 x 49 x 143 cm, W 6-16 cm / 9. wall in front of a wall in front of a wall in front of a wall in front of a wall in front of a wall in front of a wall in front of a wall in front of a wall in front of a wall in front of a wall in front of a wall in front of a wall in front of a wall in front of a wall in front of a wall, plaster blocks in front of plaster blocks in front of plaster blocks in front of plaster blocks, white 100 x 179 cm. W 40 cm / 10. floor above a floor above a floor above a floor above a floor above a floor above a floor above a floor above a floor above a floor, concrete floor on concrete floor on concrete floor on concrete floor, brown carpet on brown carpet on brown carpet on brown carpet 96 x 188 cm, W 12.5 cm / 11. ceiling below a ceiling below a ceiling below a ceiling below a ceiling below a ceiling below a ceiling below a ceiling below a ceiling below a ceiling below a ceiling below a ceiling below a ceiling, wood on a wooden construction, 160 x 196 cm, W 16 cm, ca. 200 cm distance to the ceiling below the ceiling below the ceiling below the ceiling / 12. water container in a wall in front of a wall in front of a wall in front of a wall in front of a wall, glass 12 x 12 x 12 cm / 13. room inside a room inside a room inside a room within a room inside a room inside a room inside a room, breeze blocks in a wooden construction, 2 doors in front of 2 doors in front of 2 doors in front of 2 doors, 1 lamp, tiles, wooden door in front of wooden door in front of wooden door in front of wooden door, brown carpet on brown carpet on brown carpet on brown carpet, brown wooden ceiling under brown wooden ceiling under brown wooden ceiling under brown wooden ceiling, yellow walls in front of yellow walls in front of yellow walls in front of yellow walls, furnished, detached 88 x 102 x 110 cm. W 40-48 cm / 14.

blue sheet of paper on top of a blue sheet of paper on top of a blue sheet of paper on top of a blue sheet of paper in a wall inside a wall inside a wall inside a wall / 15. room inside a room inside a room inside a room within a room inside a room inside a room inside a room, breeze blocks in a wooden construction, plastering, concrete floor above concrete floor above concrete floor above concrete floor, white walls in front of walls in front of walls in front of walls and ceiling below ceiling below ceiling below ceiling 74 x 56 x 130 cm, W 40- 48 cm / 16. doubled room inside a room inside a room inside a room: room inside a room inside a room inside a room within a room inside a room inside a room inside a room, plasterboards and a wooden construction, 2 doors in front of 2 doors in front of 2 doors in front of 2 doors, 1 window in front of 1 window in front of 1 window in front of 1 window, 1 lamp, grey floor above grey floor above grey floor above grey floor, white walls in front of white walls in front of white walls in front of white walls and ceiling below ceiling below ceiling below ceiling 135 x 174 x 168 cm, W 7.2-84 cm / 17. room inside a room inside a room inside a room within a room inside a room inside a room inside a room, plasterboards on a wooden construction, 1 lamp, grey carpet on grey carpet on grey carpet on grey carpet, white walls in front of white walls in front of white walls in front of white walls and ceiling below ceiling below ceiling below ceiling ca. 59 x 162 x 186 cm / 18. wall in front of a wall in front of a wall in front of a wall in front of a wall in front of a wall in front of a wall in front of a wall in front of a wall in front of a wall in front of a wall in front of a wall in front of a wall in front of a wall in front of a wall, plasterboards on a wooden construction, white 333 x 546 cm, W 48 cm / 19. wall in front of a wall in front of a wall in front of a wall in front of a wall in front of a wall in front of a wall in front of a wall in front of a wall in front of a wall in front of a wall in front of a wall in front of a wall in front of a wall, chalky sandstone and mortar, white 90 x 200 cm, W 48 cm / 20. wall in front of a wall in front of a wall in front of a wall in front of a wall in front of a wall in front of a wall in front of a wall in front of a wall in front of a wall in front of a wall in front of a wall in front of a wall in front of a wall, plasterboards on plasterboards on plasterboards on plasterboards on a wooden construction, white 167 x 240 cm, W 24 cm / 21. room inside a room inside a room inside a room within a room inside a room inside a room inside a room, concrete, plaster blocks, wood, l window in front of 1 window in front of 1 window in front of 1 window, 1 lamp, carpet on carpet on carpet on carpet and ceiling below ceiling below ceiling below ceiling in brown, walls in front of walls in front of walls in front of walls in white 557 x 694 x 562 cm!!! / 22. wall in front of a wall in front of a wall in front of a wall in front of a wall in front of a wall in front of a wall in front of a wall in front of a wall in front of a wall in front of a wall in front of a wall in front of a wall in front of a wall in front of a wall, plaster blocks, 1 window in front of 1 window in front of 1 window in front of 1 window, white 257 x 262 cm, W 40 cm / 23. entrance-hall, wall in front of a wall in front of a wall in front of a wall in front of a wall in front of a wall in front of a wall in front of a wall in front of a wall in front of a wall in front of a wall in front of a wall in front of a wall in front of a wall, plasterboards on plasterboards on plasterboards on plasterboards, wooden construction, light yellow, 1 door in front of 1 door in front of 1 door in front of 1 door 332 x 335 cm, S 40 cm / 24. big white door, wall in front of a wall in front of a wall in front of a wall in front of a wall in front of a wall in front of a wall in front of a wall in front of a wall in front of a wall in front of a wall in front of a wall in front of a wall in front of a wall, plasterboards on plasterboards on plasterboards on plasterboards, wooden construction, light yellow, 1 white door in front of 1 white door in front of 1 white door in front of 1 white door 333 x 580 cm, W 40 cm / 25. ceiling below ceiling below ceiling below ceiling beneath a ceiling below a ceiling below a ceiling below a ceiling below a ceiling, wood on a wooden construction, brown 67 x 85 cm, W 20 cm / 26. part of a wall in front of part of a wall in front of part of a wall in front of part of a wall in front of a wall in front of a wall in front of a wall in front of a wall in front of a wall in front of a wall in front of a wall in front of a wall in front of a wall, plasterboard on plasterboard on plasterboard on plasterboard on wood, white 67 x 40 x 27 cm / 27. part of a wall in front of part of a wall in front of part of a wall in front of part of a wall in front of a wall in front of a wall in front of a wall in front of a wall in front of a wall in front of a wall in front of a wall in front of a wall in front of a wall, plasterboards on a wooden construction, light yellow 80 x 223 x 10 cm / 28. wall in front of a wall in front of a wall in front of a wall in front of a wall in front of a wall in front of a wall in front of a wall in front of a wall in front of a wall in front of a wall in front of a wall in front of a wall in front of a wall in front of a wall, plasterboards on plasterboards on plasterboards on plasterboards on a wooden construction, light yellow 197 x 313 cm, W 20 cm / 29. room inside a room inside a room inside a room within a room inside a room inside a room inside a room, plasterboards on plasterboards on plasterboards on plasterboards on a wooden construction, plastering, 1 door in front of 1 door in front of 1 door in front of 1 door, 3 windows in front of 3 windows in front of 3 windows in front of 3 windows, 2 lamps, grey wooden floor above grey wooden floor above grey wooden floor above grey wooden floor, white walls in front of white walls in front of white walls in front of white walls and ceiling below ceiling below ceiling 207 x 426 x 152 cm, W 7.2-224 cm / 30. cube in a cube in a cube in a cube a wall in front of a wall in front of a wall in front of a wall in front of a wall, wood on a wooden construction 40 x 60 x 51 cm! / 31. wall behind a wall behind a wall behind a wall behind a wall behind a wall behind a wall behind a wall behind a wall behind a wall, black stone in a wall in front of a wall in front of a wall in front of a wall in front of a wall, plaster 9 x 21 x 9 cm / 32. soil, lead, glass wool, sound-absorbing material in the room inside the room inside the room inside the room, 2 wooden constructions, 1 door in front of 1 door in front of 1 door in front of 1 door, wall in front of a wall in front of a wall in front of a wall in front of a wall in front of a wall in front of a wall in front of a wall in front of a wall in front of a wall in front of a wall in front of a wall in front of a wall in front of a wall in front of a wall, plaster blocks, white 100 x 200 cm, W 40 cm / 33. wall in front of a wall in front of a wall in front of a wall in front of a wall in front of a wall in front of a wall in front of a wall in front of a wall in front of a wall in front of a wall in front of a wall in front of a wall in front of a wall in front of a wall in front of a wall in front of a wall, plasterboards on plasterboards on plasterboards on plasterboards on a wooden construction, white 498 x 315 cm, W 20 cm / 34. room inside a room inside a room inside a room within a room inside a room inside a room inside a room, plasterboards on plasterboards on plasterboards on plasterboards on a wooden construction, 1 door in front of 1 door in front of 1 door in front of 1 door, 5 windows in front of 5 windows in front of 5 windows in front of 5 windows, 6 lamps, grey door, white walls in front of white walls in front of white walls in front of white walls and ceiling below ceiling below ceiling 796 x 370 x 157 cm, W 7.2-132 cm / 35. moving ceiling below ceiling below ceiling beneath a ceiling below a ceiling below a ceiling below a ceiling below a ceiling, fibreboards on fibreboards on fibreboards on fibreboards on a wooden construction with wheels, 1 engine, white 271 x 354 cm / 36. three walls in front of 3 walls in front of 3 walls in front of 3 walls in the middle of the room inside a room inside a room inside a room, plasterboards on plasterboards on plasterboards on plasterboards on a wooden construction, white 303 x 400 cm, W 48 cm, 300 x 400 cm, W 48 cm, 300 x 400, W 48 cm / 37. wall in front of a wall in front of a wall in front of a wall in front of a wall in front of the entrance inside the entrance inside the entrance inside the entrance, plasterboards on plasterboards on plasterboards on plasterboards on a wooden construction 275 x 396 cm, W 16 cm / 38. walls in front of walls in front of walls in front of walls in front of a wall in front of a wall in front of a wall in front of a wall in front of a wall in front of a wall in front of a wall in front of a wall in front of a wall, plasterboards on plasterboards on plasterboards on plasterboards on plasterboards on a wooden construction 585 x 331 cm, W 16 cm, 340 x 331 cm, W 20 cm / 39. corridor inside a corridor inside a corridor inside a corridor in a room inside a room inside a room inside a room, plasterboards on plasterboards on plasterboards on plasterboards on a wooden construction, 1 lamp, brown floor above brown floor above brown floor above brown floor, white walls in front of white walls in front of white walls in front of white walls and ceiling below ceiling below ceiling 52 x 77 x 185 cm, W 4, 32-48 cm / 40. wall in front of a wall in front of a wall in front of a wall in front of a wall in front of a wall in front of a wall in front of a wall in front of a wall in front of a wall in front of a wall in front of a wall in front of a wall in front of a wall, plasterboards on a wooden construction with wheels, 1 white door in front of 1 white door in front of 1 white door in front of 1 white door 238 x 318cm, W 44 cm / 41. rotating room inside a room inside a room inside a room within a room inside a room inside a room inside a room, plasterboards and chipboards on plasterboards on plasterboards on plasterboards on chipboards on chipboards on chipboards on a wooden construction with posts and wheels, 1 engine inside another engine inside another engine inside another engine, 2 doors in front of 2 doors in front of 2 doors in front of 2 doors, 1 window in front of 1 window in front of white window in front of 1 window, 1 lamp, 1 cupboard, grey wooden door in front of grey wooden door in front of grey wooden door in front of grey wooden door, white walls in front of white walls in front of white walls in front of white walls and ceiling below ceiling below ceiling, detached, ca. 35-105 cm distance to the outer room inside a room inside a room inside a room, window in front of window in front of window in front of window looking south 107 x 132 x 170 cm, W 7.2-140 cm / 42. 1 window in front of 1 window in front of 1 window in front of 1 window looking north, 1 window in front of 1 window in front of 1 window in front of 1 window looking west, wall in front of a wall in front of a wall in front of a wall in front of a wall in front of a wall in front of a wall in front of a wall in front of a wall in front of a wall in front of a wall in front of a wall in front of a wall in front of a wall, plasterboards on plasterboards on plasterboards on plasterboards on a wooden construction, window in front of window in front of window in front of window, white 236 x 315 cm, W 7.2-132 cm / 43. wall in front of a wall in front of a wall in front of a wall in front of a wall in front of a wall in front of a wall in front of a wall in front of a wall in front of a wall in front of a wall in front of a wall in front of a wall in front of a wall, plasterboards on plasterboards on plasterboards on plasterboards on a wooden construction, 1 window in front of 1 window in front of 1 window in front of 1 window, white 236 x 315 cm, W 7.2-132 cm / 44. part of a wall in front of part of a wall in front of part of a wall in front of part of a wall in front of a wall in front of a wall in front of a wall in front of a wall in front of a wall in front of a wall in front of a wall in front of a wall in front of a wall, plasterboards on plasterboards on plasterboards on plasterboards on wood, white 98 x 128 x lo cm / 45. part of a wall in front of part of a wall in front of part of a wall in front of part of a wall in front of a wall in front of a wall in front of a wall in front of a wall in front of a wall in front of a wall in front of a wall in front of a wall in front of a wall, plaster block on plaster block on plaster block on plaster block, white 10 x 10 x 10 cm / 46. 3 parts of a wall in front of 3 parts of a wall in front of 3 parts of a wall in front of 3 parts of a wall in front of a wall in front of a wall in front of a wall in front of a wall in front of a wall in front of a wall in front of a wall in front of a wall in front of a wall, breeze blocks and plastering on plastering on plastering on plastering, white 65 x 343 x 10 cm, 51 x 343 x 10 cm, 30 x 254 x 10 cm / 47. 2 parts of a wall in front of 2 parts of a wall in front of 2 parts of a wall in front of 2 parts of a wall, pillars in a room inside a room inside a room inside a room, breeze blocks around wood, white 21 x 337 x 22 cm / 48. part of a wall in front of part of a wall in front of part of a wall in front of part of a wall beneath the ceiling below the ceiling below the ceiling below the ceiling, plasterboards on wood, white 14 x 474 x 250 cm / 49. wall in front of a wall in front of a wall in front of a wall in front of a wall in front of a wall in front of a wall in front of a wall in front of a wall in front of a wall in front of a wall in front of a wall in front of a wall, breeze blocks and plastering on plastering on plastering on plastering, white 345 x 689 cm, W 40 cm, 40 cm / 50. room inside a room inside a room inside a room within a room inside a room inside a room inside a room, plasterboards on plasterboards on plasterboards on plasterboards on a wooden construction, 4 doors in front of 4 doors in front of 4 doors in front of 4 doors, 1 lamp, brown wooden floor above brown wooden floor above brown wooden floor above brown wooden floor, white walls in front of white walls in front of white walls in front of white walls and ceiling below ceiling below ceiling 54 x 70 x 141 cm, W 7.2-120 cm / 51. wall in front of a wall in front of a wall in front of a wall in front of a wall in front of a wall in front of a wall in front of a wall in front of a wall in front of a wall in front of a wall in front of a wall in front of a wall in front of a wall, plasterboards on plasterboards on plasterboards on plasterboards on a wooden construction, white 164 x 261 cm, W 24 cm / 52. 6 walls in front of 6 walls in front of 6 walls in front of 6 walls behind a wall behind a wall behind a wall behind a wall behind a wall behind a wall, plasterboards on plasterboards on plasterboards on plasterboards on a wooden construction, plastering on plastering on plastering on plastering, white each: 90 x 205 cm, W 48 cm / 53. wall in front of a wall in front of a wall in front of a wall in front of a wall in front of a wall in front of a wall in front of a wall in front of a wall in front of a wall in front of a wall in front of a wall in front of a wall in front of a wall, breeze blocks and plaster blocks, plastering on plastering on plastering on plastering, white 272 x 259 cm, W 40-48 cm, 8 cm / 54. distance to the wall in front of a wall in front of a wall in front of a wall in front of a wall / plastering on plastering on plastering on plastering, white 65 x 55 cm, W 44 cm / 55. guest room inside a guest room inside a guest room inside a guest room, 2 layers of lead on 2 layers of lead on 2 layers of lead on 2 layers of lead, 3 layers of glass wool on 3 layers of glass wool on 3 layers of glass wool on 3 layers of glass wool, 1 layer of rock wool on one layer of rock wool on one layer of rock wool on one layer of rock wool, 1 layer of sound-absorbing material around a room inside a room inside a room inside a room, 3 wooden constructions, plasterboards on plasterboards on plasterboards on plasterboards and plastering on plastering on plastering on plastering, 1 door in front of 1 door in front of 1 door in front of 1 door, 1 lamp, 1 pit, 1 grey wooden floor above 1 grey wooden floor above 1 grey wooden floor above 1 grey wooden floor, white walls in front of white walls in front of white walls in front of white walls and ceiling below ceiling below ceiling, detached 156 x 301 x 199.5 cm, W 48-400 cm!!! / 56. inner shell deconstructed / room inside a room inside a room inside a room within a room inside a room inside a room inside a room, breeze blocks and plaster blocks, concrete floor with a puddle above concrete floor with a puddle above concrete floor with a puddle above concrete floor with a puddle, cement plastering, 1 door in front of 1 door in front of 1 door in front of 1 door, 1 lamp, grey walls in front of grey walls in front of grey walls in front of grey walls, ceiling below ceiling below ceiling and floor above floor above floor above floor / wall in front of a wall in front of a wall in front of a wall in front of a wall in front of the entrance, breeze blocks and plastering on plastering on plastering on plastering, closed box inside closed box inside closed box inside closed box, white 150 x 246 cm, W 48 cm / 57. wall in front of a wall in front of a wall in front of a wall in front of a wall in front of wall in front of a wall in front of a wall in front of a wall in front of a wall, breeze blocks and plastering on plastering on plastering on plastering, white 536 x 447 cm, W 48.5 cm, ca. 85.6 cm distance to the wall in front of a wall in front of a wall in front of a wall in front of a wall / 58. room inside a room inside a room inside a room within a room inside a room inside a room inside a room, breeze blocks and plasterboards, wood, plastering on plastering on plastering, 3 windows in front of 3 windows in front of 3 windows in front of 3 windows, 20 lamps, brown wooden floor above brown wooden floor above brown wooden floor above brown wooden floor, white walls in front of white walls in front of white walls in front of white walls and ceiling below ceiling below ceiling, detached 289 x 810.5 x 300.2 cm, W 48.80

cm / 59. room inside a room inside a room inside a room within a room inside a room inside a room inside a room, plasterboards and chipboards on a wooden construction, plastering on plastering on plastering on plastering, 3 doors in front of 3 doors in front of 3 doors in front of 3 doors, 4 lamps, 1 mirror ball, wooden floor above wooden floor above wooden floor above wooden floor, red carpet on red carpet on red carpet on red carpet, white walls in front of white walls in front of white walls in front of white walls and ceiling below ceiling below ceiling, detached 50 x 270 x 180 cm, W 4.8-40 cm / 60. room inside a room inside a room inside a room within a room inside a room inside a room inside a room, plasterboards and chipboards on plasterboards on plasterboards on plasterboards and chipboards on chipboards on a wooden construction with posts, 2 doors in front of 2 doors in front of 2 doors in front of 2 doors, 1 window in front of 1 window in front of 1 window in front of 1 window, 1 lamp, 1 radiator, floor of lead sheets above floor of lead sheets above floor of lead sheets above floor of lead sheets, grey carpet on grey carpet on grey carpet on grey carpet, white walls in front of white walls in front of white walls in front of white walls and ceilings below ceilings below ceilings below ceilings, detached, ca. 30-50 cm distance to the outer room outside the room outside the room outside the room 187 x 323 x 252 cm, W 6-48 cm / 61. room inside a room inside a room inside a room within a room inside a room inside a room inside a room, breeze blocks in a wooden construction, plastering on plastering on plastering on plastering, 1 door in front of 1 door in front of 1 door in front of 1 door, concrete floor above concrete floor above concrete floor above concrete floor, white walls in front of white walls in front of white walls in front of white walls and ceiling below ceiling below ceiling, detached 44 x 52 x 90 cm, W 48 cm / 62. wall in front of a wall in front of a wall in front of a wall in front of a wall behind a wall behind a wall behind a wall in front of a wall in front of a wall in front of a wall in front of a wall, plasterboards on plasterboards on plasterboards on plasterboards on a wooden construction, 1 window in front of 1 window in front of 1 window in front of 1 window, white 240 x 351 cm, W 50-140 cm / 63. wall in front of a wall in front of a wall in front of a wall in front of a wall behind a wall behind a wall behind a wall in front of a wall in front of a wall in front of a wall in front of a wall, plasterboards on plasterboards on plasterboards on plasterboards on a wooden construction, white 60 x 351 cm, W 50 cm / 64. ceiling above a ceiling above a ceiling above a ceiling above a ceiling above a ceiling above a ceiling, fibreboard in front of fibreboard in front of fibreboard in front of fibreboard on wood on top of wood on top of wood on top of wood, white 340 x 450 cm, W 10

I enter the house inside the house inside the house inside the house inside the house alone.

I make my way through

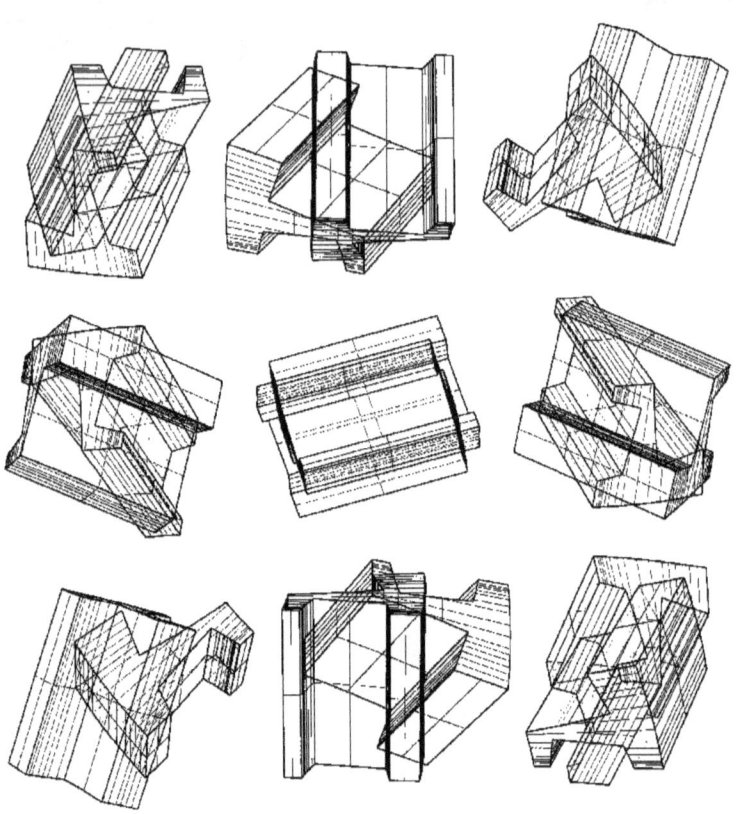

POSTSCRIPT

They say there's no record of my ever visiting *Die Familie Schneider*, that the keys were issued only through formal bookings and my name does not appear on their list. I say, Kafka wrote *Amerika*, didn't he? You know, without ever leaving Prague. But this just pisses them off, I can tell. I might as well be talking to my parents, who managed to reimagine an entire world without ever leaving their house.

I do remember a room made from corrugated iron with a floor drain. I don't remember seeing any blood, but I do remember imagining traces of it everywhere. I do remember a small pink mattress leaning against the far wall.

I recall reenacting a murder by digging up the remains of ten young girls who had been tortured to death and eating them. I find several shallow graves under the floor of my child's basement playroom. Whatever residue there is here is too persistent simply to cover up with a new basement floor or a fresh patio.

Horror is an inventory of objects, only some of which are inanimate. Don't we all have to observe despairing routines? What is life anyway but repetitions observed to forestall the superstition that you will otherwise die. Nobody's humanity is quenched in a house like this, in a house inside a house like this...

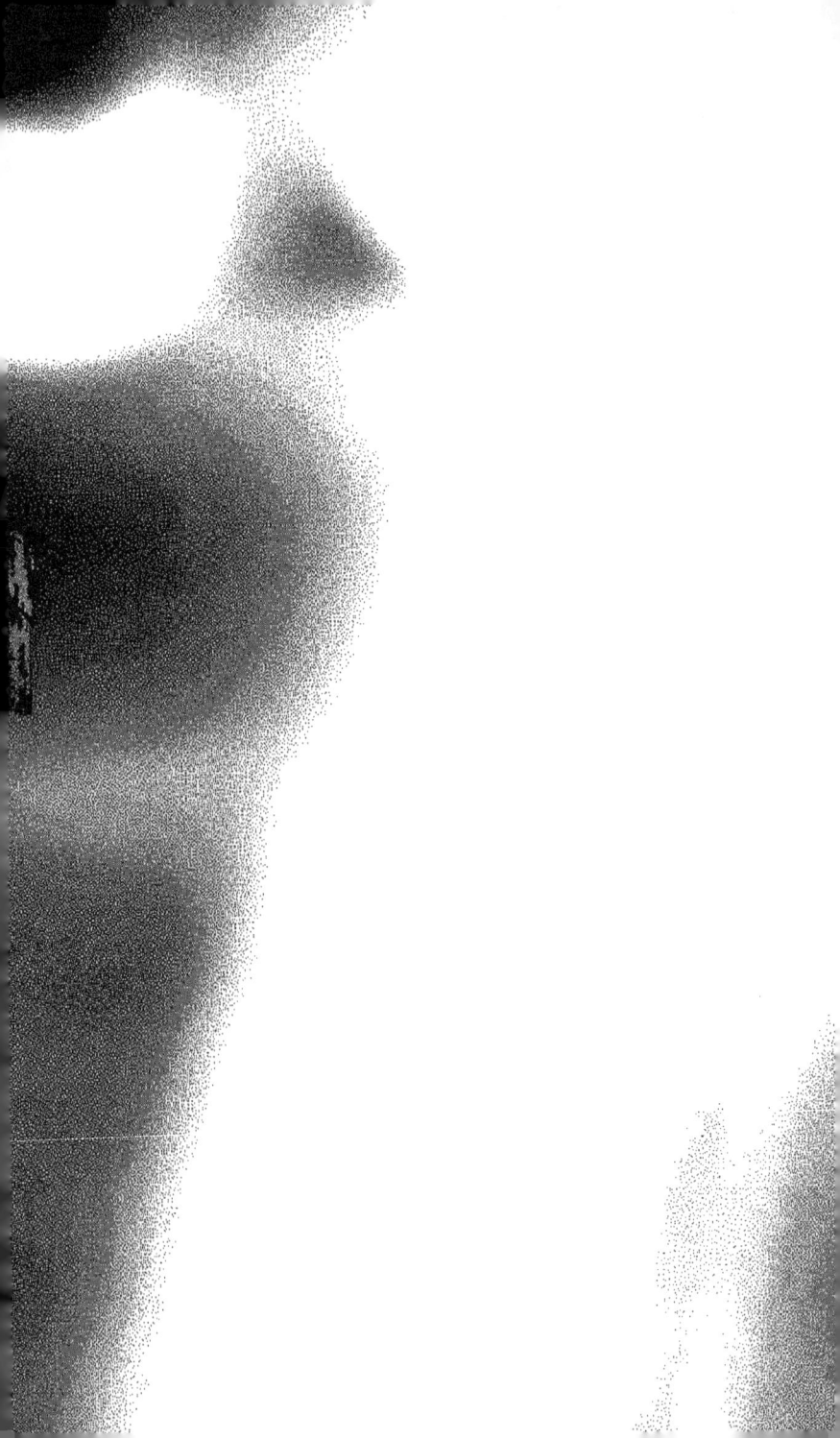

www.ingramcontent.com/pod-product-compliance
Lightning Source LLC
LaVergne TN
LVHW041800060526
838201LV00046B/1060